Tavish's heart dropped. "That's not… I didn't know I'd be working with you when I offered."

Beans whirred in the grinder. She stared at the counter and gripped the machine as it slowed into silence, didn't move to add the coffee to the French press on the opposite counter.

"I figured you'd be so busy at the clinic that we'd barely see each other." He offered the excuse in a gentle voice.

"Whatever." Lauren swallowed audibly and circled the island to stand close enough to him that she had to tilt her chin to look him in the eye. He had a good foot on her, something she'd always complained about. Why, he didn't know. It had just made it easier for him to pick her up, pin her against a wall and send her into oblivion. Her fresh-from-the-shower scent drifted into his nostrils, a hint of tropical summer and sugary sweetness. His mouth watered. Just one taste would do it.

* * *

SUTTER CREEK, MONTANA:
Passion and happily-ever-afters in Big Sky Country

Dear Reader,

Do you have a "one that got away"? The person whom you collided with, kissed, loved—then had to let go? In *From Exes to Expecting*, a year has passed since homebody Lauren and globetrotting Tavish shared a secret Vegas wedding, and a more secret divorce. But a piece of paper can't erase years of being drawn to each other.

When a family wedding pulls Tavish back home, the last thing he's prepared to do is face Lauren across a church aisle again. And the nine-month surprise that follows what they vowed would be one last night together? It rocks the foundations on which they've constructed their miles-apart definitions of *home*.

I grew up in a small town nestled between the mountains and the ocean, so Sutter Creek's outdoorsy, close-knit vibe comes from deep in my heart. *From Exes to Expecting* is my debut novel—I'm thrilled to share it with you. Stay tuned for the second and third installments in the Sutter Creek, Montana trilogy.

I would love to hear your thoughts about the Dawsons and their little mountain town. You can find me on Facebook, Twitter and at www.laurelgreer.com.

Happy reading,

Laurel

From Exes to Expecting

Laurel Greer

HARLEQUIN® SPECIAL EDITION

Recycling programs
for this product may
not exist in your area.

ISBN-13: 978-1-335-46565-8

From Exes to Expecting

Copyright © 2018 by Lindsay Macgowan

This edition published by arrangement with Harlequin Books S.A.

For questions and comments about the quality of this book, please contact us at CustomerService@Harlequin.com.

Printed in U.S.A.

Raised in a small town on Vancouver Island, **Laurel Greer** grew up skiing and boating by day and reading romances under the covers by flashlight at night. Ever committed to the proper placement of the Canadian "eh," she loves to write books with snapping sexual tension and second chances. She lives outside Vancouver with her law-talking husband and two daughters. At least half her diet is made up of tea. Find her at www.laurelgreer.com.

To Rob and our Bear and Mouse.
A lot of family juggling took place for this book
to get written, and I'm immeasurably grateful
for the sacrifices made and support given
to have my dream come true. I love you.

Chapter One

Sneaking out the back door is self-preservation, not bad form, right? Biting her lip, Dr. Lauren Dawson glanced at the clock on the wall of the Sutter Creek Medical Clinic's staff lounge. Five-oh-one. Yup, skedaddle time. After working a series of six-day weeks, her body ached for the cushy lounge chair on her lakeside deck. Getting to start her long weekend while the late-May sun still had heat left in it was worth the faux pas of creeping out without saying goodbye. She threw her leather flats into her messenger bag and slid on her flip-flops.

The door to the lounge creaked behind her. Her stomach sank and she stared into her locker, not wanting to turn around. If it was one of the nurses coming to nab her to treat another patient, she'd—

"Lauren. Glad I caught you before you left. Do you have a minute?"

Damn it. The longer she lingered, the higher the

chance of getting asked to cover drop-ins for an extra hour or two. But no way could she slough off a conversation with the man who held the future of her career in his hand. Squeezing her eyes shut for a second, she forced a smile and faced her boss. "Hi, Frank."

The fluorescent lights of the staff lounge yellowed Frank Martin's gunmetal-gray hair as he took a seat on one of the couches arranged into a conversation pit. "Quitting time?"

Lauren nodded and pulled off her lab coat. "Yeah. Andrew's still very understaffed at work, so I'm picking up some slack for him this weekend. He's got his bachelor party, so he's asked me to cover some zip-line tours, and I'm helping his fiancée with some wedding stuff." As the Director of Safety and Risk Management and the head of summer operations for their family's Montana ski resort, her older brother did more than his fair share of boosting their bottom line. Lauren pitched in where she could despite the clinic's tendency to consume her waking hours. Once her summer holidays started in six weeks, she'd be subbing for her brother, letting him get away on his honeymoon. "Pretty sure I won't get a moment to myself for most of the weekend. Though I'm hoping for a few hours to myself tonight. My dock is calling me."

His mouth curved in understanding. "Well, I won't keep you. But I wanted to make sure you got the partnership papers from your lawyer."

Those cursed papers sat on her kitchen table, mocking her every morning as she ate her oatmeal and berries. Mocking her commitment to follow in her mother's footsteps. Dampness bloomed on her palms. She'd wanted to have a practice in her tiny hometown since she was fourteen. Getting to buy in to the clinic her mother had founded was nothing less than her childhood dream. *So why am I having so much trouble putting my signature on the contract?*

She mentally flicked away the doubt and nodded at her boss. "Yeah, but I've run into a glitch getting the funds released from my grandparents' trust. My lawyer's busy arguing with their lawyers." She gripped the strap of her bag and took a centering breath. Ugh, what she'd do to have her vacation starting today. Both the wedding and working for Wild Life Adventures would be a welcome change of scenery. She would get outside for a few weeks and come back to the clinic refreshed and ready to make her plan a reality.

"Did your lawyer indicate how long it would take to fix the problem?" Concern edged Frank's words.

"She wasn't specific, no. I'm sure it'll be dealt with by the time I'm back from my holidays in July."

"That's two months from now."

Swallowing her nerves, she nodded. "It's not affecting the work I can do, though. So I'm hoping the delay isn't a deal breaker."

"No. Nothing you can do about banking complications." He drummed his fingers on the arm of the couch. "I've been waiting for this for a long time, Lauren. Having a Dawson as a partner again is going to fill a void. You'll be a great permanent addition to the clinic."

Permanent.

Normally a calming concept, but Lauren's heart started to thud as if she were sprinting. She inhaled. Her mother had been proud of her calling. And Lauren was nothing if not a mirror of her mother.

She'd almost given up on their dream once. Never again. She could do this. Was meant for it.

Her heartbeat slowed, but the burn in her stomach refused to subside.

One of the nurses poked her head into the lounge. "Dr. Dawson? Can you take one more patient before you leave? Sutures. Exam room two."

Son of a— Keeping her curse from spilling out, Lauren nodded to the nurse. She returned her satchel to her locker and shrugged back into her lab coat. "Count me there."

Frank touched his brow in a playful salute. "We'll talk later, Lauren. See you Tuesday."

"Have a good Memorial Day." Lauren changed back into her flats, straightened her khaki capris and rushed out of the lounge to her patient. Stupid long weekends and the abrasions and lacerations that came along with them. She picked the clipboard out of the Lucite holder and glanced at the patient file.

Her already complaining gut lurched and the font blurred on the page.

No. N-fricking-O.

Feet frozen two feet from the door, out of view from the patient inside, she stared through the door frame. Only the patient's legs were visible, golden-tan skin over defined calf muscles. Muddy biking footprints marked up the white linoleum. A two-inch-thick black tattoo ringed one ankle. At first glance, it looked like a series of interwoven spirals, but she knew closer study would reveal the second and third stanzas of *Do Not Go Gentle Into That Good Night*. Even marred by a fresh, index-card-size scrape, she'd recognize Tavish Fitzgerald's legs anywhere. Difficult not to, given the nights she'd spent sliding her toes along those hard calves while he'd driven her out of her mind with ecstasy.

She leaned against the hallway wall and swallowed. He must be in town for her brother's bachelor party. So much for him not coming home until a day or two before the wedding. The wedding where Lauren would have to once again stare at Tavish across the aisle. But as the maid of honor this time.

Not the bride.

Lauren's brother was marrying Tavish's sister on the Fourth of July weekend, and Lauren was thrilled to be getting a sister-in-law. She just didn't want to have to see her ex-husband in the process.

Telling herself to get a Godzilla-size grip, she stuck the clipboard between her knees and took the time to redo her ponytail. After a quick wipe under her eyes to check for afternoon mascara remnants, she clutched her clipboard between both hands, threw back her shoulders and marched through the doorway.

A millisecond after she met Tavish's gaze, her bravado tumbled into a heap around her feet. He regarded her with a simmering look as he lounged in the patient's chair next to the examination table. His violet-blue irises pierced through her layers of preservation.

Eyes that color were wasted on a man. Ditto his thick, dark eyelashes and the sun-streaked, tawny hair he never bothered to keep tidy. A navy bandanna, rolled to a hand-width and tied around his forehead, kept the windblown strands from falling in his face. He wore a technical shirt and baggy cargo shorts over black Lycra bike shorts. It was enough to make a woman's heart stop.

But no, Lauren's pulse went into overdrive, thumping loud enough she'd have worried he could hear it except she knew was it impossible. Shrinking under his silent observation, she forced herself to snap into medical mode.

"You did a number on your leg," she said.

Shrugging, he shot her a half smile. "An unruly pine."

Judging by the scrape on his left cheek, the rip in the short sleeve of his shirt and the bandage on his arm, the tree reigned victorious. His chart noted that he needed stitches for a laceration already dressed by one of the mountain first-aid attendants, but her hands were shaking so badly she didn't trust herself to pick up a needle quite yet, no matter how quickly she wanted him out the door.

"Tree, one, you, zero?" She forced out the joke.

"Yeah. Blew a tire. Landed in a snowberry bush, thankfully. Could have been worse. But where are our manners? Afternoon, Dr. Dawson." He bit out her last name.

She flinched at the emphasis. Considering she'd once shared his last name and his bed, the use of her professional title seemed overkill. "Seems silly to bother with the formalities with me."

"You're working. I respect that."

"I don't think it matters where we are. I'll always be just Lauren to you." Her voice came out way softer than she'd intended. Fighting the need to get closer to his hard, muscled body, to offer to kiss him better, she broke her gaze from his and methodically counted the eleven parts of the ear illustrated on the poster over his shoulder.

"You're never *just* anything, Lauren."

The rough sincerity in his voice chafed at her still-raw heart. She froze, not able to look at his face, to see whatever emotion accompanied the sweet words. She grabbed a pair of latex gloves from one of the cabinets and pointed at the examination table. "Up on the bed."

By the quirk of his mouth, the potential double entendre wasn't lost on him. Mercifully, he left it alone and lay down as asked, stretching out his lean frame and propping his head with his good hand.

Pulling her stool alongside him, she positioned his injured forearm for the best access. With tentative fingers, she peeled back the rectangle of gauze and recognized her brother's handiwork in the immaculate row of butterfly strips holding together the finger-length gash. The sterile material of her gloves did nothing to block the effect of touching Tavish. The moment her finger-tips brushed his arm, the heat there threatened to melt the glove to her hand.

Ignoring her pathetic physical response, she continued undoing the bandaging. "Your sister's going to smack you for getting scraped up so close to her big day. You should've held off on bodily harm until after the wedding."

Lifting his other hand across his face to touch his abraded cheek, he tilted his lips in a sheepish smile. "I wanted to try a few of the new expert trails in the biking complex. Drew took me."

"You took my brother on the double blacks? You're as bad an influence on him as you were on me." Her chest panged with immediate regret. Way to bring up how he'd made her want to veer so sharply from her life plan. To cover up her folly, she blurted, "At least he wasn't idiotic enough to tackle a tree."

Something crackled behind Tavish's eyes. Probably not the medical tape tugging on the golden hairs of his arm, either.

"You really want to get into this, Laur?" His voice held threads of warning twined with wariness.

No, but probably best to hash things out before the wedding. "We're due."

"I'd rather wait until you aren't in arm's reach of a needle." He glanced at the syringe on the rolling tray, gritting his teeth as she fussed with his laceration.

"Fine with me." She took a breath and shoved the curious blend of shame, wanting and need for escape to the back of her mind. Only in rare situations would

she choose suturing over a conversation. Wouldn't be
the first time Tavish had her doing something that went
against instinct, though. "You're going to need quite a
few stitches to make sure this heals properly. The edges
are snagged pretty badly."

"Bled like a scalp wound, but doesn't really hurt."

She rolled her eyes and readied the syringe. "You're
such a guy."

"You used to like that about me," he said under his
breath.

"Used to." She draped the wound and closed her eyes
for a second, just long enough to push away the nausea
that rippled whenever she had to pierce someone's skin.
Frustration flared over the surging acid. She'd learned
to control her gag reflex back in the first month of medical school. But the minute her lawyer had given her the
partnership papers to sign, it had come back with a ven-
geance.

Clenching her hands into fists, she breathed until her
ears stopped buzzing and she was no longer on the verge
of losing the BLT she'd had for lunch. Then she grabbed
the needle.

Tavish sucked in a breath and looked away as Lauren worked to numb the area. His brief display of nerves
made her hand itch to put down the needle and caress
his cheek. She ignored the ridiculous impulse and finished her task.

"Let that set. I'll be back in five."

"Not going to stick around and chat?"

"I have things to do."

His lips twitched with saddened amusement. "Don't
let me get in your way."

Half standing, she settled back onto her stool, meeting the challenge in his voice. "You're not in my way."

"That's not the honest Lauren Dawson I know."

She stared at him, trying to make her expression as unreadable as possible. "Fine. It's weird having you in town. And if you're insisting on small talk, where've you been since you were last home? When was that, March?" Not like she'd counted the fifty-seven days. Not purposefully, anyway.

Tavish's expression flattened into impatience. "Here and there. New Orleans for a few weeks. Italy. Brazil."

"You're definitely living your dream." If only he'd been that committed to her. To them.

"Isn't that the point?"

"Obviously. I'm doing the same."

"Sure about that?"

"Even more than when I signed our divorce papers." Though she'd had as much trouble scrawling her signature on that as with the documents for the clinic partnership. "I saw your Peru spread in *Traveler* last week."

"Make you want to go there?"

She shook her head. "Not hardly."

"Right." A visible flicker of defeat made his mouth twitch. "It wouldn't."

"I'm happy here, Tavish." *Damn it.* He'd made her defend her choices one too many times.

"Yeah, now you are. A year ago you were ready to come see the Great Barrier Reef with me."

The truth of that smacked her in the face. Tears welled at the reminder of how her grandparents' accident had turned her family upside down, had forced her to admit how her marriage would never work. Blinking away the moisture, she probed the edges of his wound. "This hurt?"

Not meeting her eyes, he shook his head.

She flushed the gash, biting her lip as saline-thinned blood trickled under the drape. *Hold it together, Lauren.*

"I traveled enough as a kid. I'm good for life." Why couldn't he understand that being rooted in Sutter Creek didn't stifle her as it did him? Besides, she had explored the globe in the past six months—via gorgeous, full-color magazine spreads. Vicarious living courtesy of Tavish himself. She'd bought every issue featuring his work.

The wearied lines in his forehead told her he hadn't changed his opinion about her choices, but he didn't bother arguing further.

"Breathe," she soothed, not liking the strain marking his stubbled jaw. "This won't take long." Thankful for something to focus on aside from the reasons her marriage had failed, she began to suture his wound.

"Getting stitched feels so weird. You probably live for this, though."

Ha, right. She'd be happy if she never saw blood again. A necessary evil, though, in getting where she wanted to be career-wise. "Don't look if it makes you sick."

"I can't not."

"Ah. You're one of those. Common enough."

"Glutton for gore, I guess."

"Checking off all the guy-stereotype boxes today."

Conversation died as she continued her stitches, a neat row of fifteen. Once finished, she dressed the wound and examined his scrapes. "I'm surprised my brother didn't cover up your other abrasions. He's the most anal medic on the mountain."

"I told him not to. I've had road rash so many times, it's second nature."

"It's your face."

He sent her a wry smile. "Worried I'll wreck my good looks?"

More like worried his good looks would wreck her sanity.

She shook her head. "We need to give each other space."

"I'll do my best to stay out of your hair until I leave town. I'm taking off on Sunday—I have jobs lined up until the wedding."

She'd have to learn to pretend ambivalence in his presence by then. She wouldn't let their ruined marriage impact Mackenzie and Andrew's ceremony. "How long are you going to be in town that weekend?"

"Five days." The blank look on Tavish's face gave away nothing. "But, look, Sutter Creek's not that small, right? We won't be in each other's pockets."

Ugh. Sutter Creek was exactly that small. But she appreciated his optimism. "You haven't spent that much time at home since college."

"I know. But I have to, for Mackenzie's sake. You're okay with it, right?"

"It's been a year." Last May, embarrassed by her failure, she'd hidden her short marriage and speedy divorce from her family. The soul-sucking lie of omission ate at her daily. She never wanted to lie to a person she cared about again. And as much as she didn't want to, she more than cared about Tavish.

He stared at her, eyes stark with honesty. His cheek flinched. "This still gets to me."

So not admitting I agree with that one. Lauren brushed a thumb across his jaw, under the abraded skin. She wished she could chalk up the pang of concern to her Hippocratic Oath. But she knew better. "You winced. I'll get you a cold pack for your face."

Giving a one-shoulder shrug, he tossed her a smile. A delicious smile. One he'd used mercilessly when he'd spent hours with his mouth on her breasts. On her stomach. Everywhere. "Don't worry about me, sweetheart."

The careless endearment hung in the air long after he left the room.

She propped her elbows on the table and took the weight of her head in her hands. She could feel the imprint of his words on her skin.

Don't worry about me...

That was the problem with Tavish Fitzgerald. She did worry about him—not for his sake, but for hers.

...sweetheart.

Knowing he'd be in Sutter Creek for the next couple of days, her muscles twitched with a sudden, and long-absent, urge to run away from home.

The last thing Tavish felt like doing after locking horns with the living reminder of his divorce was to go to a bachelor party to celebrate someone else's impending bliss. And offering to pick up the happy groom from the Sutter Mountain base lodge did nothing to help clear his mind of the woman he'd never been able to love like she deserved. The minute he set foot into the rubber-floored hallway next to the ski school, he was thrown back to the summer he'd graduated high school. How many times had he sneaked kisses with Lauren in the staff lounge? He'd worked for Sutter Mountain Resort in his junior and senior years, teaching skiing in the winter and rock climbing in the summer. The work had been awesome. So had finding excuses to flirt with Lauren up at reception.

And if he was going to have even half a chance of enjoying Drew's bachelor party tonight, he needed to get his mind off his high school girlfriend. His wife.

Ex-wife.

Trudging down the hall, he jammed his hands into the

pockets of his jeans. The movement tugged on his bandaged forearm, making him wince. Making him think of Lauren again, of her struggle to stay unresponsive while she'd sutured his cut. Her cheeks had gone all pink and... *Stop it.* She'd been holding back distaste, not desire. He shoved open the door to the ski resort's safety department headquarters. "Greetings."

"Hey." Drew, alone in the room, sat at his desk with his fingers in his dark brown hair. "Get stitched up?"

"Yeah." He rolled his shoulder, hissing at the soreness caused by his dismount into the shrubbery. "Your sister did her level best to chastise me—us—for our stupidity."

"Not surprising. Have a seat."

"Uh, where?" Tavish blinked in surprise at the disastrous state of the office. Outdoor equipment and first-aid supplies covered every surface in the place. During the winter, the office served as the headquarters for Sutter Mountain Resort's safety department. In the summer, it was the nerve center for Wild Life Adventures—or WiLA, as the staff nicknamed it—which offered everything from zip-line tours to rafting adventures. Drew and Mackenzie were damn proud of Sutter Mountain's success. Even though it was one of the smaller resort towns in Montana, they'd been operating at capacity for the last five years. And his friend would be run over by the paraphernalia involved in all that success if he didn't find a minion to organize his crap quick. "Tough to find office lackeys these days?"

"With both Zach and Mackenzie out of the rotation I had to promote my lackeys," Drew grumbled.

"Raw deal. Still, no way should you still be working at seven on a Friday. We should get going. There's a line of shots on the bar at the Loose Moose with your name on it."

"I need another ten minutes."

"All right. It's your party. Guess we'll be fashionably late." Tavish eased his way past a stack of paddles leaning against a shelf and threw himself into the chair behind the other desk. He linked his hands behind his head and leaned back in the cushy leather seat, propping his booted feet on the corner of the desk. The seat springs complained with a metallic squawk.

The complaint from Drew was a hell of a lot more colorful. He yanked off his reading glasses and tossed them onto a stack of invoices. His eyes lit a livid blue. Put Lauren and her brother side by side and he'd barely be able to recognize them as siblings. Lauren, with her blond hair and hazel eyes, resembled their late mother. But temperwise, the Dawson siblings shared a hair trigger.

"Quit it." Drew spat the words out.

"What, this?" He leaned back again, eliciting one more metal-on-metal grind from his chair for emphasis. He shot his friend a cocky grin. "Invest in some WD-40. Problem solved."

"Funny, lubricating the chairs hasn't been a priority." He waved a hand around the office. "We're so short-staffed I barely have time to sleep. I need to find a replacement for Zach or else I'm going to lose it."

"Shouldn't you have replaced him months ago?" Drew's assistant had been injured in a brutal ski accident during spring takedown and had been off since. Add in Tavish's sister being almost seven months pregnant, and Drew was short two of his most experienced guides.

"I *thought* I'd be able to cover for him. Once Mackenzie started showing, she pretty much took over as my assistant in Zach's stead. But he had a setback with his rehab. He won't be back to work until well after the wedding. And without him—or someone to work in his place—Mackenzie and I won't be able to go on our honeymoon." Drew pressed his fingers into his temples.

"Jeez. Getting married makes you overdramatic."

The other man glared before turning back to his computer. "You offering to step in?"

Tavish snorted.

"Then shut it. I'm just emailing a few buddies in Colorado who might be able to help me out. Then we can go."

Him, work in Sutter Creek? *Ha. Right.* Tavish was about as capable of that as his father had been. Even if he didn't have plans to hop on a plane to Alaska on Monday—which he did—there would be no way he could cover for Zach once Andrew and Mackenzie were out of town. Being in Sutter Creek had always made him itchy to leave. Adding his divorce to the mix made that nagging itch intolerable.

But I have a few weeks off after the wedding. And Drew's in quite the bind.

Not wanting to look too closely at the strain lines on his friend's face, he stared at the ceiling and tapped his fingers against the arms of the chair. It would be super crappy if his sister couldn't go on her honeymoon. She'd been talking about the two-week retreat to a nearby spa resort for months. The baby was due to arrive at the end of the summer, meaning it would be a long while before Mackenzie and Drew could get away again.

Tavish couldn't imagine holing up in Sutter Creek with a kid and a wife. When he and Lauren had married last year, it had been because she'd decided to leave Sutter Creek behind, to split time between his assignments and her volunteering internationally. He just wasn't built to stay in one place for long.

Two weeks, though. That would be a heck of a present for Mackenzie. Better than the set of wedding portraits he'd planned on taking for her. Ignoring his conscience as it chomped a hole in his stomach lining, Tavish picked up a pencil to doodle on a piece of scrap paper. "What kind of work?"

"Supervising sites, occasional guiding. Assistant crap."

"Maybe I could help out." He'd have to avoid Lauren, but that wouldn't be hard. She was married to her job at the clinic.

"Uh…you're not the most reliable. No offense."

Tavish bristled. Knowing he was genetically incapable of sticking around Sutter Creek for any length of time was one thing. Having his best friend confirm it was another. "No, man, I think it would work. I'll leave Monday to hang out with the polar bears, then come back for your wedding, hit on the bridesmaids—"

"Hey! My sisters are the bridesmaids."

"Right. Sorry. Scratch that. Still, I'll pitch in here and be gone the minute you're back."

Drew didn't need to worry about his sisters' honor when it came to Tavish. Given Tavish's relationship with Lauren, he'd never seen Cadence, the baby of the family, as eligible. And Lauren? Well, tried and failed there.

Seeing her today had made his brain spin, a clicking whir not unlike the ancient slide projector of his grandmother's that he credited with getting him hooked on photography. Except instead of pictures of his mother being schlepped across the country in her family's old woody station wagon, the images that flashed across his brain starred Lauren's creamy skin against white hotel sheets and the lights of the Las Vegas Strip glinting off the gold band on her left hand. A gold band Drew knew nothing about. Tavish had promised to keep that secret, even though hiding something so monumental from his best friend made him feel like a pile of bear crap.

And when he'd promised secrecy to Lauren, he'd also made a promise to himself—that he'd stop thinking about his ring on that gorgeous hand that somehow knew just the right way to grip him.

More than that—she had a total grip on his heart.

Helping out Mackenzie and Drew ran the risk of having to fight those thoughts from surfacing daily. Hourly. But what kind of brother would he be if he didn't facilitate a final kid-free trip for his sister?

"I can't let Mackenzie give up her honeymoon. She's already had to compromise by rushing the wedding. Thanks to your not having paid attention during tenth-grade sex-ed," Tavish added lightly.

A crumpled-paper ball bounced off his head.

"Asshole. But you're serious about filling in, aren't you?" Drew asked.

He nodded, curving up one side of his mouth in his own disbelief. "It's been a while since I've been able to help Mackenzie."

"It's been a while since you've been *willing* to help her, you mean."

Ouch. The accusation reverberated in his chest. He rubbed at the resulting ache. "Guess I can't argue with that."

Drew blew out a breath. "Add on the few days you'd be here before the wedding and you'd have to be in town for over two weeks. You sure about that?"

Tavish picked up a hunk of shale that served as a paperweight and passed it back and forth between his hands. "Thanks for the math lesson, but I know what I'm offering."

"Do you still have your EMT cert?"

"Yeah. I'm not stupid enough to enter war zones without knowing what to do in an emergency," he said. "Warning—this offer will self-destruct in five seconds unless you accept it."

Drew tugged at the collar of his polo shirt. "Okay, then. I'll fill Lauren in on the plan tomorrow. She'll be relieved, to say the least."

Every cell in Tavish's body froze. "Huh?"

"Well, you'll be replacing Zach, but Lauren's replacing me. Looking forward to it, or so she says. So you'll be helping her out."

Clenching his fist around the rock, he resisted the impulse to hurl it through the glass pane of the hallway door. Working with Lauren would kill him. She'd consider his involvement the antithesis of help. And he couldn't back out of the commitment now. If he did, Drew would ask questions.

Lauren's inevitable freak-out when her brother informed her would also result in raised eyebrows. Better to avoid any possibility of suspicion. "She and I should start communicating about how I'm going to best support her while you're gone, so let me tell her."

Drew shrugged. "Whatever. I'm just happy that Mackenzie doesn't have to go on our honeymoon without me." His smile turned wicked. "Two weeks of being alone."

"Dude. Sister."

"Dude," his friend mocked. "You have to know what you're facilitating."

"I know you have to shut up about it."

Mackenzie better enjoy her holiday. Because by making the most important woman in his life happy, he'd be making the woman who should have owned that title miserable.

Chapter Two

Lauren woke up on Saturday morning and reveled in not having set an alarm. Clear sky glowed blue through the skylights in her loft bedroom, promising a cloudless morning. And she planned to enjoy her three days of freedom. Freedom from blood, freedom from needles. She wasn't free from her contract, but at least with the financial glitches she could drag her heels a little longer before signing in triplicate. And her 10:00 a.m. date to help Mackenzie make chair decorations and center-pieces all but guaranteed she'd be able to steer clear of Tavish. No way tulle pew bows and glass vase arrangements would capture his interest. He barely stayed still long enough to snap pictures on the ultra-fancy camera habitually slung on his shoulder.

He was happy enough to be still when we were snuggling in bed together.

Swallowing the lump that formed in her throat, she

shot out from the covers. Her plush featherbed and Egyptian cotton sheets felt way too much like the bed they'd shared during their honeymoon in Las Vegas. She needed to clear her Tavish-and-work-filled brain with some fresh air before she headed into town to meet Mackenzie. Throwing on a sports bra, thin jacket and cropped leggings, she jogged downstairs.

Wanting her space to reflect the outdoors, she'd decorated the spacious, cathedral-ceilinged main floor in soft moss and earth tones to complement the green visible through the expansive panes of glass at the front and rear.

She loved it.

Never wanted to leave.

Her gaze landed on the thick manila folder on her reclaimed-barnwood dining table. Damn. *Usually* never wanted to leave. But the house was full of specters this morning. She'd fled the enchanting reminders of nights tangled in Tavish, only to run headlong into her work anxiety. She needed to get away from that contract before it sprouted legs and chased her around the butcher-block island.

Yoga on the dock. Yes. An excuse to leave the house without feeling like a total chicken.

Crisp forest air pricked her sinuses as she opened the glass French doors and toted her yoga mat down the stairs to the long wooden raft. The sun had risen far enough above the lush pines on the opposite bank to lend a hint of warmth to the light breeze. She sat cross-legged on her mat and stared at the ripples marring the surface of the water.

Living out on Moosehorn Lake, a twenty-minute drive from the town center, gave her enough distance not to feel truly pathetic about the double knots keeping her tied to home. She was close enough to take care of her dad and her sister, and to help Mackenzie and Andrew once the baby arrived, but far enough away she wasn't living in their pockets.

She was independent. Owned a stunning, green-roofed log house on a pristine chunk of waterfront. Had a meaningful job that connected her to her mom. So what if she chose to be a homebody, to put her family first? Just because her chosen lifestyle was the polar opposite of Tavish's didn't make it any less valid.

Though it does mean we shouldn't have exchanged rings...

And shouldn't have made promises neither of them was capable of keeping.

She was stretching into downward dog when the roar of a ski boat broke through her meditative breathing. Teenagers, probably. Her nearest neighbor, the quintessential get-off-my-lawn sort, would be pissed off to have boat noise before eight.

A quick glance west corrected her assumption of the age of the perpetrators. She immediately recognized not only the stripe down the side of the sleek vessel barreling in her direction, but the passengers within it.

Not teenagers.

Clearly the groom had escaped any serious abuse at the bachelor party if he was on the lake at this hour. The early-morning sun silhouetted her brother's broad shoulders as he steered from his perch on the top of his seat. Mackenzie's red ponytail blew in the wind from her position in the bow seat, facing backward as the spotter. Cadie snuggled in the passenger seat across from Andrew, the hood of her zippered sweatshirt pulled up.

Lauren didn't need to look to know who they were towing.

Every muscle stood out on Tavish's wetsuit-clad body

as he tore up the water behind the boat, creating an incandescent rooster tail taller than his six-foot frame.

So much for steering clear of him.

All four of them waved as they passed Lauren, seemingly headed for the slalom course a few hundred yards east of her dock.

Giving up on yoga and ready for any entertainment that could distract her from the little voice in her heart that said things she didn't want to hear, she pulled her knees up to her chest.

Her brother aimed his boat through the two white marker balls. She shadowed her eyes and reluctantly admired Tavish as he passed through the course, creating an S pattern as he cut around the balls positioned on alternate sides of the center guides.

She'd have accused him of showing off, but he had perfect right to do so. Tavish Fitzgerald carved up the water like a four-star chef did a Christmas turkey.

Something hot and needy, something she didn't want to acknowledge, pulled at her core and made her skin tingle. She rubbed at the goose bumps on her arms and tried to focus on his skill rather than his amazing body.

After Tavish successfully rounded all six obstacles, Andrew slowed the boat and Tavish sank into the water. Cadie unhooked the tow rope and reattached it at a shorter length, and Andrew kicked the boat up to a roar once again.

Tavish didn't look as competent with less rope to deal with, bailing hard after two passes. Lauren's breath caught in her throat until she heard his laugh echo on the water. Andrew didn't waste any time getting Tavish back up and heading in the direction of her dock.

She cursed her brother's efficiency. Tavish in a wetsuit five hundred yards out had heated her to the point of needing to jump in the chilly lake. Said man, plus said wetsuit, but minus four-hundred and ninety-nine yards might get her on the evening news for proving spontaneous combustion wasn't a myth.

The boat ripped by, and he let go of the rope. He was nice enough not to spray her. As a teenager, he'd been able to drench the entire public dock without getting his hair wet. She imagined he hadn't lost that talent. Then again, had he sprayed her, it might have saved her a load of embarrassment by killing the flush she knew had crept up her cheeks. He knew how to read her. Would know what her pink face meant.

Lauren bent down at the edge of the dock to catch his ski and shook her head in disbelief. "The lake's freezing and the sun is barely up."

"I don't see any ice." With a powerful stroke, he pushed his ski toward her. It skimmed into her waiting hands.

He climbed up the ladder just as she lifted the ski out of the lake, bringing her gaze within inches of the pull of his violet eyes.

She straightened, breaking away from the hypnotizing effect he had on her brain. "You're not supposed to get stitches wet. Plus, the strain could tear them."

"Drew and I made a waterproof dressing."

"And tearing?"

He grinned cockily. "I'm a risk taker."

They were interrupted by the rumbling of the boat as Andrew maneuvered it up to the dock and cut the engine. He turned down the dial on the stereo, lowering the volume on the country song blasting out of the speakers by half.

She smiled at her brother, then shook her head at Tavish. "You're a dumbass."

Tavish laughed and scrubbed the water from his hair. A few chilly droplets landed on Lauren's cheeks. She was surprised they didn't evaporate on contact.

"Nice welcome there, Laur." Andrew raised a teasing eyebrow as he shoved up his sunglasses.

"One of the many services I provide." Lauren grinned. Mackenzie tossed her the bow rope and she fastened the length around one of the cleats.

"We figured you wouldn't be busy," Mackenzie said as Andrew hopped out of the boat and proceeded to offer both his hands to help her to the dock. "We can hold off on the pew bows for an hour or two. Garnet's covering for Andrew this morning."

An hour or two. Doable. Right?

But Lauren had been wrong about Tavish one too many times to believe her own bravado.

Smiling stiffly at her siblings, she tried to ignore her ex-husband as he peeled off his wetsuit.

She failed miserably. There were things a girl could forget in her life. Tavish's ripped abdominals, marred only by a faded appendectomy scar, didn't qualify. But they didn't look exactly the same as they had the last time she'd seen him shirtless—a tattoo wrapped his torso under his left arm, a watercolor nature scene bleeding out of a bold diamond-shaped frame. The bottom of the frame dipped below the waistband of his navy-and-white surfing shorts. The scene looked familiar, but she couldn't place it. She fought the urge to reach out and trace the outline from mountain peak to stream.

Admiring Tavish's taut stomach, another urge built deep in Lauren's belly.

She fought that, too.

Mackenzie tossed him a towel, and he dried the water

droplets clinging to the butterscotch-colored hair sprinkled on his well-formed chest.

Lauren jerked her gaze away. "Cadie, is Ben with Dad?" she asked, referring to her sister's baby son.

Her sister nodded. "They headed off to see some of the new horses at Auntie Georgie's ranch for the day." Doting on Ben became a downright family competition at times. Parenting solo had been that much harder given Cadie had been recently widowed when Ben was born, so everyone pitched in when they could. "We brought chocolate croissants, Laur. Thought we'd have a bite to eat and then do some more skiing."

Accompanied by Tavish's perfectly formed pecs. Great. Drawing from the same well of determination as when she dealt with bodily fluids at the clinic, she forced her lips into a grin and reached for the box of pastries. "I'll take these up to the patio table and go put on a pot of coffee. Want me to boil some water for herbal tea, Kenz?"

"Please," Mackenzie replied, eyes slightly narrowed. She'd glanced between Tavish and Lauren more than once since getting out of the boat.

Lauren beat a hasty retreat to her kitchen. She had to do a better job of hiding her reactions to Tavish over breakfast.

For the next twenty minutes she sipped her coffee, munched on a croissant and participated in small talk. She even did a decent job of keeping her eyes on her food and off the way Tavish's arms bulged under his T-shirt.

Setting down his empty coffee cup with emphasis, Andrew looked at her with a cheeky smile. "You going to try to beat my slalom-course record today, Laur?"

"I just may." She grinned back, feeling in her element for the first time since Tavish showed up for stitches yesterday. Skiing, she could do. She ran into her house to grab her wetsuit and skis, early hour and ex-husbands be damned.

When she returned, Cadie and Mackenzie had taken up residence in the pair of cushioned lounge chairs on the dock. Her brother sat sideways in the driver's seat of his boat, sandals propped on the passenger's dashboard. Tavish straddled the port-side gunwale, one bare foot in the boat and one on the dock. All long limbs and straining T-shirt and way too delicious.

As Lauren strolled down the gangplank with her ski in one hand and her life jacket in the other, she caught him watching her. His throat bobbed. Yeah, she knew she looked good in her wetsuit. The neoprene enhanced each one of her curves. A thrill zipped through her body that he'd noticed.

"I'm up next," she announced. "I want to see what my new ski can do."

"I think it's more the skier than the ski, Laur." Tavish raked a hand through his hair. Sunlight reflected off the twisted gold-and-silver links of a bracelet on his left wrist. "When was the last time you went out?"

"Last weekend." She walked to the end of the dock, watching him with a confident eye as she sprayed lubricant in the bindings and slid her feet in.

"I don't remember you being that into waterskiing," he said, sounding puzzled.

She mimicked the cocky grin he'd sent her way when he'd skied up to the dock. "That's what happens when you stay away—people change. And learn how to trounce you on the slalom course." She sat on the edge of the dock, both feet secure in midcalf-high boots, and held her hand out for the tow rope.

"You want this length?" Tavish's eyes widened. The

rope was still the length he'd last used—one requiring a good deal of skill.

"For now. I'll use it as a warm-up."

He guffawed. "A warm-up. Right."

"Yeah. Right." She left no room for misunderstanding in her voice.

"Okay." He didn't sound at all convinced as he tossed her the rope and sat on the passenger side of the boat with his feet resting on the carpeted engine cover.

Andrew turned to Tavish. "Ten bucks says you eat your words."

Tavish snorted. "Done."

Within a minute they roared away from the dock. Lauren channeled her frustration over Tavish's doubt into cutting back and forth across the wake until they entered the slalom course. Then all thoughts of her ex-husband disappeared as she focused on leaning against the rope, flying back and forth. Releasing her outside arm as she rounded each ball, then pulling the rope in tight to her hip as she turned in the other direction, she did her best to send up a cascade of water twice the size of Tavish's.

As she cut around the third ball of six, she let out a whoop—she'd beaten Tavish's performance. *Ha.* Her competitive streak hadn't kicked in this strong in a while. She'd blame him for that, too. He was already at fault for stealing away the peace of her morning; what was one more charge?

Successfully reaching the end of the course, Lauren held up a palm in a stop signal. Andrew slowed the boat to an idle, and she sank into the water.

"Take the rope in, Tavish," she called.

"Seriously?" His voice lifted in surprise. "Twenty-eight feet off is damn tough."

"And I'm damn good." Satisfaction spread through her

at being able to bring the glow of amazement into Tavish's eyes. "Change the rope. And hurry up. Pretty sure I can feel ice crystals in my capillaries."

"Don't get testy. I just didn't know you were trying to go pro." Tavish unhooked the rope and refastened it, six feet shorter.

"I beat you. Now I need to do the same for Andrew." Lauren took a breath and gripped the rope handle. She'd have to stretch out parallel to the water to get around any of the balls—her five feet and one scant inch worked against her at this point.

"Ready, Lauren?" Andrew called.

"Hit it." Lauren tucked and let the boat pull her out of the water.

She quickly adjusted to the short rope. The heat of temper buzzed in her muscles as she stretched out toward the first ball. Releasing the handle with one hand, she cut around the obstacle. Inches from the surface of the lake, she somehow managed to pull herself up with enough time to repeat the feat on the other side. Her arms and quads screamed at her. She forced her body to submit one last time but that was it. Muscles totally gassed, she ripped back toward the middle of the wake where she stayed instead of trying for the remaining balls. That tied her brother's personal best—she'd beat him by the end of the summer. And surpassing Tavish tasted too sweet to fuss about Andrew's record. Tapping her head with the palm of her hand to signal she wanted to head home, she made lazy passes all the way back to the dock.

Cadie and Mackenzie clapped loudly as she let go of the rope and sank into the water. She shimmied out of her ski and propelled it toward Cadie, who waited for it on the dock. "My turn!" her sister announced, getting ready to enter the water.

Tavish climbed out of the boat, and Mackenzie took his place as spotter, and then Andrew gunned the engine once more.

Lauren busied herself drying off and slipping back into her yoga pants, not happy to be left alone with her ex-husband, who stood by the ladder. With his back to her and his arms crossed, she could only guess that he was feeling the same. But she wasn't in a hurry to find out if she was right on that. The out-in-the-wide-open dock smothered like a musty closet.

By the time she acknowledged him with a quiet "Pretty sure you owe Andrew ten bucks," the boat was at the far end of the lake.

Sitting on one of the lounge chairs, he stretched out his long legs. He linked his fingers behind his head and fixed her with an inquisitive look. "You trying to prove something out there?"

"Maybe." She sat down on the other deck chair and snuggled against the backrest. "Guess I wanted to remind you that just because I'm a homebody doesn't mean I'm boring."

He stared at her for a few seconds, shaking his head. "Pixie, I haven't had a boring moment with you once."

Pixie? Oh, God. He'd started calling her that back in high school once he'd officially surpassed her by a full foot. It had made her laugh then, so she'd put up with it. After she broke up with him—college plus distance did not mix—he'd stopped using the endearment. Until he and Andrew had crashed her friends-only trip to Vegas to celebrate her finishing her residency. He'd confessed to still loving her, to wanting to make it work. And she'd loved him enough to try to compromise. Once they'd exchanged vows, he'd added "Pixie" back into his lexicon.

Usually when he was trying to get her out of her clothes.

Then again, "I love you" had worked like a charm, too. But it had only taken a couple of weeks to learn no compromise was enough to keep that love alive.

He pressed his lips together and looked away. Was he as tortured by the memory as she? He deserved to be, damn it.

"Quite the place you found," he ground out.

Glancing up at the sparkling glass and stained logs, Lauren smiled. "I bought it in the fall."

His eyes turned serious. "I'm surprised you're this far out of town, though. Given how you insisted you wanted to stay close to your dad and Cadie."

"Just because I want to be close to them doesn't mean I need to live next door." Glaring at him, she pressed her water-chilled hands against her too-hot cheeks.

He got a near-apologetic look on his face. "Or maybe they don't need you as much as you claim they do."

The heat in her face spread down her neck, spiraled into her belly and legs. She dropped her hands, clenched her fingers. "I'm less than a half hour away. That's pretty fricking close."

"And if we'd been somewhere else and they'd needed you, you could have—" He sighed. "Never mind. I needed to talk to you about—"

"We've done enough talking."

"I—" He shifted his gaze to the end of the lake, where the boat had turned around. The hum of the engine reached a crescendo as it approached. "I guess it can wait. So, you were pretty impressive to watch out there."

She wanted to insult his own performance to regain a fighting position in their spar, but couldn't, not when any insult would be a lie. "You, too," she admitted.

His expression flickered with amusement. "Was that so hard?"

"No." Some lies were worth the guilt. She pivoted, feeling stronger facing him head-on, and rubbed her hands together to try to increase the blood flow to her ice-cold fingertips. Sometimes she could forget, could go back to when she was seventeen and he was eighteen and they had all summer to flirt and gibe. Other times, the pain of his desertion—and the knowledge she was equally to blame as he was—hurt so badly she expected to spit up blood.

He leaned forward and took her hands in his. The warmth of his touch immediately seeped into her skin. "I didn't think we'd end up like this. I thought we'd move on."

A solid rush of frustration erupted in her chest. "How am I supposed to move on when you keep poking at me, trying to make it sound like it was all my fault we couldn't make this work?"

He sat, mouth open, gripping her hands so she couldn't get away. She pulled, but he hung on.

"Let go, Tavish. We failed at being together. And I've been lying to my family about it for a year. Two transgressions I don't take lightly."

He met her challenge with a gaze that bit straight through to her core. His grip on her fingers changed from a utilitarian warming rub to a more sensual press. "It's not something either of us should take lightly. And had you been willing to tell our families about what happened in Vegas, you might not be so damn stuck."

"I am not stuck." *And he's not going to believe me unless I stop shouting.* She lowered her volume. "What would it say about me if I didn't feel bad for lying to my family?"

"They didn't need to know. That's what you said, anyway." He traced his fingers against the backs of her hands. His touch felt too gentle, too caring, coming from someone incapable of a functional relationship. Lifting one of her hands to his lips, he kissed her fingertips, setting them off like sparklers.

"I don't need you to validate my guilt, Tavish," she snapped. Not only might their siblings be watching from the boat, but his lips plus her skin still equaled electric currents—both problems with potentially disastrous outcomes. Yanking her hands away, she stood. "I'm going to go get more coffee."

By the time she climbed the stairs to her house and entered her kitchen, all her self-preservation had drained from her like a trail of gasoline from the dock to the house, ready to ignite and burn to cinders. She poured herself a fresh mug of coffee but didn't drink, just let the heat from the pottery leach into her hands. It was a safer heat than Tavish's.

Her life felt like an "Oh, God, Dad's coming over in ten minutes and the house is filthy" moment. But she had carefully stuffed her crap into closets so no one would realize how messy she was. She'd been Cadie's sounding board since Sam died, and her father's since her grandparents' fatal car accident last May. Last May when she'd been secretly standing at an altar with Tavish. Goddamn it. Sure, Andrew was a rock, but he had Mackenzie and the baby to worry about, and couldn't always be there for Cadie and their father like Lauren could.

Somehow, she needed to construct a Rocky Mountain-size barricade between herself and her ex-husband. Gripping the kitchen counter, she stared through the window as the boat returned to the dock and everyone piled out. She relaxed at the prospect of no longer being alone with

Tavish. Until realization struck—she'd let him chase her off her own dock. *Shameful.* She stomped back down the stairs.

Cadie flopped onto a lounge chair and snuggled under a towel, and held her hands out to Lauren. "Can I hold your coffee for a few minutes? My fingers are numb."

"Sure." Lauren passed the mug over and sat down in the chair next to her sister's, trying to convince herself that the smell of sandalwood lingering on the cushion hadn't come from Tavish's soft hair. He'd climbed back into the boat and sat in one of the stern seats, concentrating intently on the screen of his cell phone. He'd zipped into a hoodie, but that did nothing to minimize his hotness—just one more article of clothing to strip off him. Getting to undress him in their honeymoon suite while he stood stock-still, eyes burning with need, had been one of the best—

Ugh. What is my problem *today?*

He stretched, exposing a thin line of tanned, tattooed skin between his hoodie and board shorts.

Thanks for the taunt, universe. That was a hypothetical question. Didn't really need the object lesson.

"Let me know when you're warmed up, Cadie," Andrew said, tugging Mackenzie into the bow seat and pulling her in close next to him. "You can drive and I'll ski back to the boat launch. After this run, I'm going to head into the office for a few hours."

"You were supposed to take the day off," Tavish said in a half-engaged tone, still focused on whatever he was reading on his cell.

"And so were you, but you seem pretty absorbed in your emails," Andrew countered.

"Yeah, just got my itinerary for my Thailand assignment in the fall."

Leaving again. Of course. She steeled herself before disappointment struck, before she wasted any more emotions on Tavish.

Turning off his phone, Tavish jammed it in his pocket. "Sorry. All yours until tomorrow."

Andrew rubbed his hands together and let out an exaggerated cackle. "Better get used to it. In no time it'll be the wedding and I'll own your ass. I think I'll start training you this afternoon so there's less to do in July."

Training? The word skittered down Lauren's spine like an unwelcome insect. She shivered and pinned Tavish with a questioning look.

He paled. "Uh, well—"

"What is going on?" Her heartbeat filled her ears, drowning out the sound of water slapping against the dock.

"Finally found you help for while I'm away," Andrew said, climbing out of the boat with an oblivious grin on his face. "Tavish is going to be your assistant."

Gripping his sandwiched-together flip-flops in one hand, Tavish smacked the rubber against his thigh and huffed out a breath. Ah, hell. That was not how he'd wanted Lauren to find out. He should have told her when he had the chance.

Turning white, she stammered out an excuse of having to have a shower before meeting Mackenzie in town for wedding prep. She sprinted up her multileveled deck as if trying to escape an encroaching forest fire.

And it was up to Tavish to put out the flames. He tilted his chin at Drew, who was sitting on the dock waiting for his turn for a ski. "You know, Lauren and I need to coordinate our best-man/maid-of-honor speeches. I'm going to stick around, throw some ideas by her. I'll catch a ride into town with her."

Drew nodded and zipped up his life jacket. He caught the tow rope from Mackenzie. "See you at the office?"

"Yeah, give me an hour." Provided he made it to town without Lauren dispatching his body on a deserted dirt road.

He hugged his sister and Cadie, ignoring the suspicion written on their faces.

A minute later the roar of the boat retreated into the distance. He stared up at the house, the one Lauren had bought and made into a home without him. Not that he needed a house. Just the opposite.

After Mackenzie had shacked up with Drew, Tavish had taken over her apartment to avoid having to find a new place to stash the few boxes of childhood mementos and photography equipment he'd been keeping in her spare closet. That served as more than enough of a base. No point in owning a chunk of property or some neatly constructed glass and logs if he wasn't ever going to be in town long enough to enjoy them.

He took a deep breath and trudged barefoot up the sets of half stairs. His knock on the glass door went unanswered, so he pulled it open and stepped into the open-concept kitchen and living area. Running a hand along the green-flecked granite counter, he blinked as his eyes adjusted after being in the bright morning sun. "Lauren? You here?"

The dining table sat empty, as did the chocolate-colored leather couches and armchairs curved around a stunning river-rock fireplace that soared all the way to the pine-planked ceiling. He let out a low whistle. Talk about a showpiece. But the house managed to look livable, too.

Touches of Lauren livened the room: clusters of family pictures and splashes of color in throw pillows and an orchid, plum and cream-striped floor rug anchoring the couches. Job hazard, noticing color. Though that didn't stop his friends from giving him grief for knowing the difference between orchid and plum. *Whatever*. The predominant moss-and-tree-bark motif made him think of curling up with a bowl of popcorn under a blanket and listening to spring rain on the tin roof. Thanks to the sudden end of their marriage, they hadn't had the chance to do normal husband-and-wife things, movies on the couch and the like. But they'd been pro snugglers when they'd dated in high school—it took zero effort to remember the comforting shape of her shoulders under his arm.

He wandered over to the mantel, to a pair of photographs in mismatched standing frames. None of him there, not that he expected it.

But he did recognize himself in one sense—he'd taken both the pictures on display. A shot of Drew, Cadie and Mackenzie laughing on a chairlift—he'd been on the chair in front of them and had turned around at the exact right time to capture the women doubled over at one of Drew's jokes. The other one, though—he had to close his eyes for a second before he could fully take in Drew and Lauren on their trip to Vegas, sitting in the center of a small group of Lauren's friends. Lauren wore a tiara, a silly gift from her brother for finishing her residency. Tavish had been working on a magazine spread in LA, so he'd joined them on impulse. And the day everyone else had left, Tavish and Lauren had exchanged rings.

"Why are you still here? Your ride's gone." She threw the accusation out from somewhere behind him.

He turned, held up his hands in mock surrender. "I come in peace."

Gripping the newel post, she shuffled her feet on the

bottom tread of the staircase. Her sleek hair hung in just-showered tendrils around her shoulders, making damp spots on her silk bathrobe. That material would be touchable as hell and, with her soft skin, it would be hard to tell where silk ended and flesh began.

Cool it, Fitzgerald.

He jammed his hands into the front pockets of his hoodie sweatshirt. "Just needed to explain myself."

"Explaining yourself is well and good, but you're getting back to town how?" she demanded.

"Uh, you?"

"Try again, Tavish." Crossing her arms over her chest, she sent him a death stare.

Okay. So his prediction he might end up in a shallow grave wasn't far off. And no way were his fingers getting even close to touching her.

Instead of verbally running in circles, he went for the easy out. He pasted a cheeky smile on his face. "That's a pretty complicated half hitch in your panties, Lauren."

"You can dream about seeing my panties, but it's not going to happen."

He chuckled. She made it so easy. "I don't need to dream, sweetheart. I got my fill in Vegas. You still like lace, or have you moved on to the waist-high, granny kind?"

"Wouldn't you love to know?"

A predictable response, clichéd even, but it pierced the bull's-eye. Discovering white lace under Lauren's wedding dress had killed him. And getting to touch her over the soft material, coaxing sexy moans from her with his fingers? The memory still kept him up at night. He barely held in a groan and ran a hand over his face before she realized just how much he'd love to delve under her robe. To find out what she had hidden beneath. Maybe nothing but her sweet skin.

"Nice house. I recognize the artwork." He jabbed a thumb toward his photography on the mantel.

"Don't read anything into it. You have a way with a camera." Her pink cheeks contrasted with her blanched knuckles, which were clenched in fists at her sides. "And with ruining my summer vacation, apparently."

"You going to give me the chance to explain before you reduce me to ash with that glare?"

"By all means." She stomped into her kitchen and started opening and slamming cabinets before yanking out a coffee canister and grinder and placing them on the granite island. Sure, her anger had grown to the point that he could almost see it shimmering on her skin, but too much white showed around her irises to peg her as solely pissed off. She was covering for something he didn't want to poke too much. Unearthing their feelings could suck him past the point of no return.

He strolled to the island and leaned his forearms on the surface across from where she was shakily scooping beans into the grinder. "Mackenzie and Drew needed help, Lauren. Otherwise they were going to have to cancel their honeymoon."

"Nice to know you're more concerned about your ex-brother-in-law than your ex-wife." She pressed her lips together, brows knitted into a near V-shaped blond line.

Tavish's heart dropped. "That's not… I didn't know I'd be working with you when I offered. And it's about my sister, too, not just Andrew."

Beans whirred in the grinder. She stared at the counter and gripped the machine as it slowed into silence.

"I figured you'd be so busy at the clinic that we'd

barely see each other." He offered the excuse in a gentle voice.

"Whatever." Deserting the coffee, she circled the island and stood close enough to him that she had to tilt her chin to look him in the eye. He had a good foot on her, something she'd always complained about. Why, he didn't know. It had just made it easier for him to pick her up, pin her against a wall and send her into oblivion. Her fresh-from-the-shower scent drifted into his nostrils, a hint of tropical summer and sugary sweetness. His mouth watered for a taste, just one...

And now he was lying to himself and not just his family. Great.

She slumped against the counter. "So, two weeks?"

The urge to touch her, comfort her, licked up his arms. He fisted his hands. "I'm sure if we schedule things right, we can avoid actually being in the office at the same time."

"That's not the problem!" She jabbed him in the chest. Her utilitarian-length nail wasn't sharp enough to dig in, but she put enough force behind it for it to sting. "I can't believe you'd step in with this, but you wouldn't stick around for me!"

He caught her by the wrist before she could poke him again. "You needed more than two weeks, Lauren."

Swiping at her eyes with the back of her other hand, she nodded. "I needed a lifetime."

"And I couldn't give that to you. Still can't." Not if it meant holing up in Sutter Creek. He ran his thumb along the fleshy base of her palm. The tendons in her hand tensed under his touch.

She glanced down at his fingers circled around her wrist, then back up to his face.

Those damp eyes. Holy hell. Through all of his travels,

the countless people he'd captured with his camera lens, he hadn't come across irises that exact blend of amber and spring green. Nor had he ever encountered eyes that could stare right to the core of his soul. A fist clamped around his stomach. He released her arm and tucked a damp wave of hair behind her ear. "That's why we cut and ran. Better for both of us."

"Was it really? Better, that is." Her lips parted and her chest rose and fell faster than normal.

"I'm betting my mom would say it was. My dad jerked her around for almost a decade—did the same to Mackenzie and me—before disappearing. Our decision seems miles more responsible."

Her expression softened, and she touched his face. Skilled physician's fingers drawing down his cheek, leaving behind a trail of aching emptiness. They settled on his left pec. Did she know she owned the organ beating under her palm? That he'd given it to her in high school, and even through long-distance breakups and divorce, he'd never quite gotten it back?

"I'm not putting all this on you, you know," she said. "I changed my mind. Was just as much at fault as you sticking to your need to roam."

He settled his hand over hers and squeezed. "Never thought you were."

"We'll get through working together somehow. Through seeing each other every day."

Anticipation, blended with dread, fused his heart to his lungs. He wanted to see her every day. And knew he'd feel like he was walking on knife blades each day he did.

"Maybe it'll help us find closure," she added.

He snorted.

"What?"

"We've wanted each other for over a decade. I don't

see that ending for me after spending two weeks watching you trot around the WiLA sites in tight technical gear."

Her cheeks pinked. Her hand still rested on his chest and her fingertips dug into the muscle a fraction. "Kind of like you showing up on my dock in a fricking wetsuit?"

"I couldn't exactly turn down the invitation when Drew extended it. Figured the fewer questions the better." Sending her a pained grin, he brushed the backs of his fingers along her jawline. "And you can't point fingers about wetsuits."

The corner of her mouth curved as she toyed with the open zipper on his hoodie, running the tab up and down the teeth. "Pretty sure Cadie and Mackenzie suspect something's going on between us."

"We'll hide it. Even if you did decide that you were ready to be honest about our marriage, dropping it on our families right before Drew and Kenz tie the knot would be the definition of unfair."

Nodding, she slid her hand under the cotton of his hoodie. It rested on his waist. What he would give for her to drop that hand lower, cup his hardening length. He closed his eyes and shifted his weight, hoping she didn't notice how much of an effect she was having on him. "I should probably go."

It would be a long walk back, especially in flip-flops, but he didn't trust himself to stay in her presence any longer without reaching for the row of tiny buttons holding the fabric of her robe snug under her breasts.

She stepped into him, until only an inch separated their bodies. A charged, heated energy thrummed between them, seeped from his skin deep into his bones. He couldn't be the first to close the space. Couldn't do that to her.

He didn't have to. Standing on her toes, she pressed a kiss just above the collar of his T-shirt. "I dunno. If we're needing closure… Maybe you should stay."

Chapter Three

Tavish sucked in an embarrassingly shaky breath. "Stay?"

"Yeah." Her lips landed on his collarbone again, along with the smallest flicker of her tongue. A fluttering, resolve-weakening caress. "Stay."

"I shouldn't." He cupped the back of her head with one palm. Taking one of her hands, he twined his fingers with hers. "But when have we ever done what we should?"

She looked at the floor, sucked in a breath and then made fierce, needy eye contact with him. "Never. And we'll be quick."

He chuckled. "I might take my time. It's been a year since I've had my hands on you, and since you're talking about closure, we won't do this again. So I'm going to savor every second."

A faint complaint escaped the back of her throat. Those flushed cheeks, the bare thread of control in her eyes—she'd be the death of him.

Settling his hands on her hips, sliding them over the slick silk, his heart stuttered. Yup, cardiac arrest city. But what a way to go.

Rocking back a step, she plucked open one of the buttons holding her robe closed on the side. The thin strip of material was the only thing keeping him from palming her soft, pretty breasts. Man, he had a backlist of ways he wanted to pleasure Lauren Dawson. Freezing in his cot in Siberia this winter, he'd compiled a mental tally of ways they could have kept warm together. He started to shrug out of his hoodie, but she stopped him with a firm look.

"I'll do that." She frantically shoved the material off his shoulders. It landed on the hardwood with a *swoosh*. "Hurry."

She flicked another one of her buttons open.

His body twitched in agreement with her command for speed. *No, slow down.* "Why so urgent?"

"To make sure we get into town on time."

"They think we're speechwriting. If we're late, they won't question us." His fingers shook as he managed to undo the rest of the delicate placket. One side of her robe fell to the side, baring a hint of supple skin, but another layer of thin material hid the rest of her. Lifting her and settling her on the counter, he groaned. "This robe is keeping me from seeing you, sweetheart. I think you did this on purpose."

"It's buttoned on the side. Inside." A sheen of sweat glimmered on her upper lip. She near to whimpered, forehead creasing with complaint, and scrambled for the bottom of his T-shirt. She tossed the material to the floor and moved on to the Velcro fly of his board shorts.

He placed a hand gently on the side of her neck, kissed the opposite collarbone. "Hold on, Laur. I don't mind speeding this up some, but I don't want to miss the next part."

Shaking, eyes closed, she paused. Clenched her hands around his hips as, with a care he'd only ever felt for Lauren, he popped a few of the hidden buttons holding her robe together. Jade lace peeked out on one side from the parted fabric. He traced a finger along the exposed material.

"Tavish." She kneaded his hips and squirmed under his touch, bucked forward. Pressed her heat into his hardening erection. He let out a loud groan and dispensed with the rest of her buttons. Her robe parted like a jacket, only a few scraps of sheer lingerie covering all the parts he wanted to touch.

Starting with her mouth. "I haven't even kissed you yet." And he'd fix that. He claimed her soft lips with his, nipped and delved and loved her mouth until the faint hint of her chocolate-and-coffee breakfast flooded every part of his tongue.

Reaching again for his shorts, she dipped her fingers under the back of his waistband and cinched her legs around his hips. Her soft center was aligned with his very need. Amazing enough on its own, but then she twisted her hips. He had to lock his knees.

"Tavish, foreplay is nice and all…"

"Nice?" He shot her a look of mock insult and reached a finger down to the lace below her navel, drew a wavy line in and out of the top inch of her panties.

"Really nice." Her chest rose and her thighs tightened around his pelvis.

Tavish's mind cleared of everything but Lauren and how good it was going to feel to bury himself in her body. He flicked open the front clasp of her bra and cupped her breasts with all the reverence she deserved, swirled his thumbs around her beading nipples. "Pixie, you are so gorgeous."

"You, too. But I want more." She framed his face in her hands, took his lips hostage and dueled with his tongue until he could barely breathe. "All of you. Now."

Within seconds of her command, one that came from a place Lauren hadn't known existed, Tavish unwound her legs from his hips. He shucked off his shorts.

Lauren was caught by his beauty. Not unawares. She knew the shape of his muscular chest, the hair that delineated the center of his abs. But having all of Tavish in front of her, having him offer himself to her, made her realize how unprepared she was. Unprepared to deal with the sum of muscles and entrancing tattoo and that sexy happy trail. And every time she tried to speed up the kissing and stroking, he slowed her down.

She didn't want to question having asked him to stay, just wanted to escape into the sensual haze. Shedding her panties, she pulled his hips back into the cradle of her own. A groan escaped from his parted lips. He played with the ends of her half-dry hair, ran his fingers through it. Seemed to savor, soak in the sensual touch.

The trees and water of his tattoo rippled, took on life. She outlined the diamond shape from the top of his rib cage, along the smooth skin of his side until she hit cotton. She nudged down the waist of his boxers, her fingers kissing the tight ridge of muscle that arrowed toward his groin. And something about the movement of his muscle under ink had her straightening. "Oh, my God. You designed your tattoo. It's your river spot."

The waterside nook, accessible only by secluded trail, where they'd last made love…

"Mmm." He licked a path along her neck, leaving behind a shivering trail of skin.

"Tavish, that means something..."

"It means I like trees." Cupping her chin, he stared at her, a wild gleam in his eyes. "Forget about my tattoo and finish taking off my boxers."

I like trees. Utter crap. But now wasn't the time. She hooked both fingers in the elastic at his waist but didn't push the fabric down. "Like this?"

Hissing his agreement, he dropped his head back, exposing tight cords in his neck. And Lord, she craved his taste, the sensation of male skin on her tongue. She nipped and laved above the notch in his collarbone. Moaned as the familiar salt and spice teased her memories.

Wanting to run from the past, she held him tighter, allowed the fever filling her body to translate into agitated strokes and squeezes.

"Come on, Tav. More."

"Shh, Pixie," he soothed.

His hands glided along her skin, like the silkiness of lake water brushing against her limbs while she floated. Every muscle fiber of his body tensed. She sensed him fighting his control, leashing the demanding desire within. Following through on his promise to torment her with slow lovemaking when all she wanted was to speed up. Slow meant feeling. Letting in emotion and eventual heartache. Her pulse jumped, sputtered. *Why, why isn't there a way to enjoy this without thinking about what it means?*

"You deserve better than a quickie on your kitchen counter, Laur," he murmured, trailing his mouth from the tiny mole on her right shoulder to the valley between her breasts. "We should go upstairs, do this right."

Her body throbbed with unspent need. Closure was one thing, but inviting him into her actual bed would only ensure she'd never be free of him. She couldn't sleep there if the memory of Tavish and his tormenting hands and tender words lay beside her. "No. I want you inside me. I want it fast. Raw. Make me stop thinking."

"Lauren." His hands hovered over her breasts, freezing inches away from her aching skin as his irises turned smoky. She closed her eyes against the onslaught of his gaze. How could he see through her so easily?

He palmed the left side of her head and pressed his mouth to just above her right ear. "You're not going to be able to use this to numb you. If that's what you're going for, we need to stop." His chest muscles went rock-solid under her hands, seemed to complain at his statement.

"Stop? As if." Shifting against his rigid, clothed arousal, she coaxed a groan from his lips. *Better*. She had to get him to stop talking. Of course it was going to hurt, but it would hurt whether they got involved or not. Right now, going over the edge with Tavish would soothe some of the tears stinging the backs of her eyes, threatening to well.

His expression, aroused but full of doubt, clouded more. "If this is going to hurt you more than you already are, Lauren…"

"You agreed to this. No crisis of conscience now." Lauren kissed him quiet, tried to erase the darkness from his gaze by brushing her lips across his eyelids. "Don't make me beg, Tavish. Not for real, anyway. I wouldn't be here, doing this, if I didn't want it."

"Okay, then," he rasped, an eagerness riding his scratchy tone. His fevered hands and lips caressed, kneaded, took her down further into the foggy heat. "Wait. We need a condom."

"Yeah. Of course." No need to admit she hadn't actually slept with anyone in the past year. Nor did she want to know if he had.

He scrambled for his wallet in the pocket of his hoodie and pulled out a foil packet.

Taking the protection, she forced his boxers off his hips and rolled it on him, then notched her body against his. She reveled in his hot length as it singed her aroused, aching folds. "Now?"

"Hell, yeah." With an agony-and-pleasure-filled breath, he lifted her, thrust to her core.

Her body spasmed, drew him in deeper. The fluid rhythm of hips and thighs and hands overwhelmed. The intimate lock of his body in hers fit closer than she remembered. How had she walked away from the feeling of being more than herself?

"Faster." She needed the now to wash away the then. Needed pure physical sensation.

No thoughts.

No memories.

And then the ache, the craving, melted into all-encompassing flight and glow. Tavish's groan and release dragged Lauren just that much further into bliss.

She held on to his shoulders, on to the brilliance, for as long as she could. But as his chest heaved up and down, she surfaced from the haze.

She'd never wanted anyone as much as she still wanted him. Yeah, they'd been good last summer.

They were spectacular now.

Her eyes closed and, despite being pressed up against his hot skin, her body chilled far faster than it should have. His head seemed to weigh a thousand pounds against her shoulder. Warning jolts shot up her spine.

Curse the physical-emotional pull still knitting them

together. And though she wished she could somehow unfurl the stitches, they were part of each other's life tapestries. A reality that had made Tavish's propensity for avoiding Sutter Creek so fricking convenient. And made his choice to sub in at WiLA a fatal threat to her heart and sanity.

Doing this hadn't provided closure. If anything, it had torn her heart open that much wider.

Chapter Four

Six weeks later

"Just the usual, Lauren?"

The bubble that had been bumping around her stomach since she woke up lurched at the idea of an iced coffee. Stupid work and wedding stress.

Eight more hours at the clinic. Then you don't have to think about it for a couple of weeks.

A thought that not only failed to calm her unsettled tummy but came with a punch of guilt for wanting to get away from work so badly. But her lawyer had called yesterday to assure her the glitch preventing her from accessing her trust had almost been ironed out. Reality loomed—in two and a half weeks, she'd return from summer holidays a full clinic partner.

Rubbing her twisting abdomen, she shook her head at the barista, Garnet James, who was waiting behind the

Peak Beans' register with a curious smile on her face. "Matcha latte today, please." *And carbs. Like, now.* "And one of the plain scones."

Mackenzie strolled over from the table she'd nabbed, fists pressed into her pregnancy-swayed back. "Make that two scones, please."

Garnet busied herself taking Lauren's payment and dishing pastries onto plates, her red curls bobbing around her face. She and Mackenzie often got mistaken for cousins, given their nearly identical hair color and all the time they spent patrolling together. Garnet worked part-time for the mountain and would soon start working for the new holistic health center that AlpinePeaks, Lauren's family's company, was opening in the fall. The woman knew her way around an acupressure table. Lauren would have asked her about nausea relief, but only someone asking for trouble would bring up morning sick—

Don't even think of calling it morning sickness. *It's nerves.*

She and Tavish had used a condom, dammit.

And she'd gotten her period since.

Two percent failure rate. And your period was really light. Like, say, spotting. And it should have showed up last weekend, too.

Growling at her inner textbook nerd and reminding herself that stress caused periods to fluctuate, she accepted her drink from Garnet.

"Kenz, next time you and Lauren come in for your Wednesday breakfast, you'll be a married lady," Garnet said.

Grinning, Mackenzie danced in a celebratory circle, then winced.

"Ligament pain?" Lauren asked.

"Oh, yeah."

Garnet wrinkled her nose. "I hear that's the worst."

Mackenzie shook her head. "I'll take the third trimester over the first any day. Sore breasts—" *Check*.

"—falling asleep standing up—"

Double check.

"—morning sickness—"

Since Monday... Oh, Jesus.

Her heart raced and spots danced on the edge of her vision.

"So, Garnet," she said in an overly bright tone, "are you excited to quit this place when the health center opens?"

"Couldn't be happier." Garnet eyed Lauren carefully. "You okay, hon? You look pale."

The back of Lauren's throat burned. She wanted to be like Garnet—happy about her new business opportunity. Also key: Garnet wasn't preg—

Don't.

—nant.

Her latte hit the floor. The lid popped off and green, milky liquid splattered her favorite suede flats and the tops of her feet. Pain flared, and holy crap, if her shoes were ruined...

"Ow," she said feebly, staring at the spreading puddle.

"Oh, hon!" Garnet exclaimed. "What happened?"

Tears pricked the corners of her eyes. "I wrecked my shoes..."

"Blakey, bring the mop, will you?" her friend called to the back of the store, hurrying around the counter with a rag.

"I love these shoes."

Mackenzie pressed the back of her hand to Lauren's forehead. "Garnet's right—you're pale. Clammy, too.

You're not getting sick before my wedding, are you? I'm afraid I won't allow that. My day has to be perfect."

Lauren swallowed. "It will be."

As long as your brother doesn't freak out and bolt when he finds out he's going to be a dad.

Fisting her hands to prevent herself from touching her stomach, she glanced between her friends, the puddle, her now-spotted shoes, poor Blake de Haan and his mop—

"I'm so sorry. I'm late." *In more ways than one.*

"Get to work," Garnet said, waving her away. "I've got this."

She croaked out her thanks and hurried for the door before she burst into tears on Mackenzie's shoulder.

Ten minutes later, she leaned against the wall of the single stall in the staff bathroom at work, a used pregnancy test clutched in her hand. It was from a box of samples a pharmaceutical company had left for the lab tech to try out. No one would notice she'd taken one.

The results of the test? Quite the opposite. In another two months or so, maybe three, she'd start showing.

And everyone would notice that.

Bracing her forearm against the cold metal of the stall, she pressed her nose to her skin in a vain attempt to hold back a sob.

A baby.

She brushed her free hand over her lower abdomen, and a swell of sheer joy flooded past the crippling shock gripping her body.

Her baby.

Not just yours. Tavish's, too.

Right. Tavish.

Would he even want to be a father? During their handful of idyllic honeymoon days, kids had come up, and neither of them had been sure if they wanted to be parents.

Awareness, deep and real and so damn right, rushed into her chest. Caring for her patients meant supporting women, no matter what choice they made about pregnancy, but for her… For her, no debate was required. The tiny bundle of cells inside her would eventually grow into a baby. One she planned to love with every inch of her being. She had the resources, support and will to be a great mom, no matter how involved Tavish decided to be.

But holy crap. She was not looking forward to that conversation. And with him returning from his assignment to start fulfilling his best-man duties—and subbing in at WiLA—tomorrow morning, she didn't have long to wait.

"Lauren!" Cadie's sharp elbow landed between two of Lauren's ribs.

Lauren jumped. Yeah, her head had been in the clouds since she took the pregnancy test yesterday morning. A justified state, she figured. However, she wasn't ready to confess the reason for her fog to her younger sister. Especially not while holding a microphone in front of the few hundred Sutter Creek residents who filled the Main Street Square for the Independence Day festival.

Cadie stood at Lauren's side with her sleeping son strapped to her chest in a baby carrier. Strands of dark hair drooped around her face, having been coaxed out of her tidy bun by the heat. Lauren knew her own ponytail wasn't in any better shape. The canopy tent overhead provided shade, but the sun was still making it impossible to look halfway decent in front of the crowd. Or, say, one's ex-husband—the one responsible for guaranteeing Lauren would be the one wearing a baby carrier come next summer.

You were there, too. You can't blame him entirely.

No, no she couldn't. She'd blamed herself almost every

minute since she took the test and went for a quick, confidential follow-up appointment with one of her colleagues yesterday to confirm the pregnancy and review her list of dos and don'ts—stick to low-impact exercise, minimal caffeine, take prenatal vitamins, etc. But she could blame him for looking fresh as a damn daisy in his teal technical shirt and climbing gear. God, had they run out of extra-large shirts or something? The large Cadie had given him was too tight. Indecent, really, snug around his cut biceps and pecs—

Thinking like that got you into this mess.

"You're forgetting to commentate," her sister chided, elbowing her again.

"Right. Sorry." Rubbing her smarting ribs, she focused on the Wild Life Adventures' rock climbing demo in front of her and held the microphone to her lips. "Tavish is getting set to challenge my brother, here. Let's see if he remembers how to do this, ladies and gentlemen…"

Was there really a best time to get life-changing news? Probably not. But this weekend counted as the worst. Tonight she was hosting Mackenzie's bachelorette party, and then tomorrow was the rehearsal, and Saturday, the wedding—

Her gut wobbled and she wiped her sweaty forehead. Unclenching her jaw, she fixed her attention on the crowd. "Holy smokes, everyone! Tavish just bested Andrew's time by a full three seconds. Guess he's managed to do some climbing in between all that picture-taking."

The audience of heat-wearied parents and children wearing star-spangled face paint seemed to like her soft jabs in the direction of their favorite famous son. Tavish might not love Sutter Creek, but Sutter Creek loved him. And given her job today was to entertain with the hope of selling more adventure packages, she'd use his reputation unapologetically.

The sun, out in full glory for the Fourth of July, beat down on the applauding crowd overflowing the grassy square at the center of town. Even after spending more than half her life in the ranching- and tourism-based town, she still loved how the historic Old West buildings blended so well with the newer shale-and-cedar architecture popular in ski towns. Homey and outdoorsy, it felt established. Close-knit. Small. Perfect for raising a child.

For raising a child alone? She gripped the microphone tighter. Sweat beaded along her hairline and made her polo shirt stick to her shoulder blades. But her internal thermostat issues were less a result of the sun and more the fault of the man who'd just raced Andrew to the top of the thirty-five-foot climbing wall. And damn it, she'd happily take the distraction. "If you'll fix your attention on Tavish—" *How could anyone not? His ass. Good Lord...* "—at the top of the wall, the guy who just showed my brother how things are done." She smirked pointedly at the crowd and garnered a laugh. "You'll see he's ready to rappel down."

She explained the technique to the crowd, barely able to focus on her words. The flex-and-spring of Tavish's leg muscles drew all her attention. That, and the fact she was currently growing an embryo he knew nothing about. *Gah.* Maybe waiting a few days to tell him wasn't so bad. It only seemed right that one of them spend the wedding weekend free of thoughts of onesies and coparenting...

The crowd applauded again as Tavish landed on the ground, took a bow.

Show off. She ignored his second bow in her direction.

Saliva built up in her throat, made her cheeks tingle, and she shoved the microphone at Cadie. Spinning, she clung to the edge of the table and heaved in a breath, willing herself not to lose her breakfast in public.

"Uh—" Cadie sputtered. "At WiLA, we offer classes from beginner to advanced, for kids and adults…" She continued on with the closing spiel and gave thanks to both the rock-climbing and mountain-biking demonstrators. Lauren owed her sister. Cadie didn't like public speaking.

A minute of slow breathing settled her body.

"What the heck was that?" Dangling the microphone in Lauren's direction, Cadie ran a hand absently over the downy hair on her son's head. Ben's cherubic face was smooshed sideways and his little mouth hung open in his can't-get-more-peaceful-than-this infant way.

That's going to be me soon. Oh, wow.

Straightening, she sent Cadie an apologetic smile. "I guess the heat's getting to me."

Climbing gear clinked, drawing her attention away from her sister. The smile slid from her face as she got sucked in by Tavish lifting his helmet from his head, sweat curling the strands at his nape. He tipped his head back with a laugh at something Andrew said.

She loved seeing him laugh. And damn it, he'd do anything but when she dropped the "dad" bomb on him. *So wait until after the weekend. He'll be happier that way.*

"Lauren!" Cadie squeezed her shoulder and followed her line of sight.

"Sorry, what?"

A dark brow curved up in suspicion. "I was saying you should go home. Take a nap before the party tonight."

"I'll be fine." She yawned. Okay, maybe a nap wasn't a bad idea. Her life was supposed to have calmed down this year. The chaos of last summer, from Cadie moving back to town after her husband's funeral to Grammy and Grandpa's car accident to Lauren's wedding-slash-divorce, had been enough for a decade. Now that she'd gotten her family more settled, this holiday should have been different. But one little word—*stay*—and she was tangled up in Tavish all over again. Would he want to be an involved parent? Or would he take off the same way he had on their marriage?

"You know, if something's on your mind, I'm here to listen," her sister offered.

"Sure. If something comes up, I'll be sure to pull out our sleeping bags and we can stay awake all night giggling about boys."

"I hope we're beyond the crying jags over failed proms and all that. Speaking of guys, though..." Cadie glanced briefly at Tavish, who was packing away climbing ropes. "Have you and Tavish picked up where you left off in high school?"

"Why would you ask that?" Lauren blurted.

"Well, you looked like you were tempted to strip his clothes off while he was climbing."

Her mouth went dry. Oh, damn. So much for covering her reaction to him. "In case you didn't notice, he's kind of ripped. But no, there's nothing going on between us." Her chest clenched. Yet another addition to her stack of lies about Tavish. The guilt grew exponentially every time. But the dishonesty was necessary: Lauren wanted to help her sister heal from her losses, not pile on to Cadie's burdens.

"You guys were good together back in the day."

"Holding on to a high school love is the pinnacle of irrationality."

"You could do with some irrationality." Blue eyes widened on a spot over Lauren's shoulder. "Oh, hey, Tavish."

Wary curiosity crossed his face as he set a stack of

plastic tubs down in the back corner of the tent. "What's that about high school loves?"

Oh, crap. He'd heard them. At least in part. "Cadie's is over there." Lauren threw out the excuse, pointing to the raised wooden sidewalk that lined the stores on the south end of the square. "Remember Brad Gillis? She broke his heart when she went to college and met Sa—"

Her sister's eyes dampened, no doubt from the reference to her husband.

Lauren mouthed a quick *Sorry*.

"We were champion heartbreakers after high school, eh, Lauren?" Cadie wrapped her arms around Ben, who was still sleeping securely in his baby carrier. She made a big show of greeting a family perusing the pamphlets at the information table.

Acid singed the back of Lauren's throat. She wanted to slough off the accusation, to assert that she hadn't broken Tavish's heart when she dumped him during her freshman year of college, but the careful mask he wore made her wonder otherwise. Her chest tightened. Swallowing her nausea and her protest, she grabbed a bottle of water from a cooler with a shaky hand and sat on a folding chair.

Tavish tracked her movements with a studied eye. Worry tweaked his already uneasy expression. His strong hand landed between her shoulder blades as he crouched on his toes next to her chair. "You okay, sweetheart?"

"Um, did you not see Cadie when I mentioned Sam? Not my finest moment."

"She's not going to fall apart because you brought up her husband." His calm, low tone only made her insides hollow out more. He took her wrist and notched two fingertips against her pulse. "Drink that water. Gotta watch for heat exhaustion in this weather."

She snatched her arm away from his grasp. "I'm a fricking doctor, Tavish. I know how to avoid heat-related illness." She didn't, however, know how to tell him the truth. And for the sake of the wedding, she wasn't going to breathe the word "baby" until she figured it out.

Chapter Five

Tavish took a swig from his bottle of local wheat beer as he watched women flock to Drew's Search and Rescue buddies on the crowded dance floor.

Built in the basement of the Sutter Creek Hotel, the Loose Moose had to be the only establishment owned by the Dawsons' company that didn't pride itself on five-star, swanky service. It earned its fifteen-year Best Bar in Sutter Creek title by serving up cheap drinks, free pool and a loud mix of country and rock music. Nothing about its decor, especially not the moth-eaten, one-eyed moose head mounted over the archway to the washrooms, deserved reward. But it had an air so familiar it remained one of the only parts of Sutter Creek that Tavish missed when he was away. And given the girls were planning some sort of classy affair for Mackenzie's bachelorette party, the bar served as a guaranteed escape from Lauren.

At the festival this morning, she'd made it exceedingly

clear she wanted nothing to do with him. And he wasn't
going to force things, not when the attention should be
on Mackenzie and Drew. Until the wedding couple de-
parted for their honeymoon, he'd make sure none of the
tension between him and Lauren spilled out from behind closed doors.

"You not going to take advantage of your proverbial
second-to-last night of freedom?" He nudged his friend
and pointed at the debauchery on the dance floor.

Drew rubbed his hand under the collar of his striped
dress shirt. "Uh, no."

"Good. I'd flatten you if you so much as looked at a
woman aside from my sister," he said cheerfully. "But
you passed the test."

"Lucky me."

"Yes, you are. Don't forget that."

"Don't plan to."

He clinked the neck of his bottle against Drew's gin
and tonic. What Drew had with Mackenzie was nowhere
near the kind of relationship Tavish was capable of having. Neither he nor Lauren had been able to compromise
enough to make their marriage work, screwing over any
chance they'd had to stay together. And if that was love,
it wasn't worth it. Wasn't much different from his father
chasing rodeo fame and forgetting he had a family at
home. How his father's wanderer gene had skipped his
sister, he didn't know. But she was like their small-town-
loving mom all the way. Not so, him. Which was a damn
boon for nurturing a career that had him exploring the
world's nooks and crannies, but not so much for main-
taining a relationship with a woman only interested in
one particular hidey-hole.

A flurry of movement from the doorway caught Tavish's eye. His sister shimmied into the bar, decked out in

a crown and an abomination of an '80s prom dress. That shade of bubble-gum pink was like a nuclear weapon against her auburn hair. A flood of glitter-decked women followed in her wake.

"What are they doing here?"

"Who?" Drew swiveled to look. A grin split his lips. "Looks like I can dance, after all." It didn't take him more than a second to shoot off in Mackenzie's direction and only about ten more to get her onto the dance floor.

Leaving Tavish with nothing to do but stare at his ex-wife. Lauren's outfit was the opposite of abominable. Dark jeans sucked tight to her toned thighs. Fastened high on her neck, a sheaf of cotton candy-colored fabric hugged her hourglass figure from her breasts to her hipbones. And then she turned.

Backless.

Un-goddamn-believable. How was he going to keep his eyes to himself when Lauren's sweet skin was exposed and begging to be stared at?

He shifted, trying to adjust to the sudden discomfort in his jeans. He'd have to face Lauren from the front tonight. Not that looking at her face and curves from that angle turned him on any less.

The women scanned the room, must have figured out there were no empty tables because they zeroed in on him in his vacated booth and sauntered over, Lauren and Cadie in the lead.

"Can we toss our stuff here?" Cadie asked, rustling for something in her purse and perching on a chair.

"By all means." He motioned to the empty booth seating and the handful of chairs he'd appropriated hours ago. Most of the women dropped their things on the vinyl bench and traipsed away to join the gyrating mass in the sunken dance floor.

Twisting her hands, Lauren glanced around as if to decide where to sit.

Jesus, no need for that. If she didn't get a hold on how awkward she got around him, the entire bar, not just their siblings, was going to start wondering what their problem was. He grabbed the wooden back of the one closest to him and pulled it out from the table. "Here. Sit."

"I— Fine." Clutching a shoulder-wrap thing in her hands, she settled on the edge of the chair.

A delicious waft of pineapple upside-down cake— perfume? Body cream?—hit his nose and he almost groaned as his groin twitched again. "Defeats the purpose of a bachelor party to bring the bride."

"Hard to say no to said bride when she starts pouting," Lauren retorted. Way too many emotions were written on her face for him to decipher. Annoyance for sure. Heartache, maybe. And a sliver of fear. His gut clenched on that last one. Didn't sit right, Lauren being scared.

"Up for a game of pool?" He tried to smile his way into her good graces.

Lauren peered at Tavish, declining with a shake of her head.

"How about a drink, then?"

"I'm the DD," she said in a rush, then seemed to check herself. "But if you're insisting, I'll have a sparkling water."

If she was going to make him work for her company, he'd play along. "Nah, I'll get you something nicer."

"Fine." Though her flat lips said otherwise.

"You want something, Cadie?"

"Just a beer, please."

"Light lager, right?"

A smile brightened Cadie's light blue eyes. "Yeah. Good memory."

Lauren's cheeks stretched in surprise. Did she not think Tavish was decent enough to remember basic facts about his friends? Ouch. He missed her faith in him, no matter how ill-deserved it had been.

And for the sake of tomorrow's rehearsal and the dinner to follow, he needed to talk her out of her jitters. "You know, I was supposed to get another drink for Drew, and I'm not going to be able to carry all that. Could you give me a hand, Laur?" Shooting her an innocent look, he cocked his head.

She opened her mouth as if to protest but rose and followed him without complaint. Careful to touch only the paltry strip of her blouse at her lower back, he guided her toward the mirror-backed bar curving against the rear corner of the room like the hip and shoulder of a guitar. No small feat. The place was packed for the holiday. A large crowd of scantily clad college girls clustered up to the bar, taking their chances on the infamous Wheel-of-Shot-Fortune. The skirts were short. The laughs were tipsy. The smiles screamed "available." He wanted none of it.

Ouch. I'm getting old.

Or, despite the impossibilities, he still wanted the woman weaving through the crowd at his side.

They lined up behind a cluster of people. Lauren nudged his hand with hers, forcing him to drop it from her back.

"It's crowded, Pixie, and you're not exactly tall. I don't want some drunken fool to elbow you in the head or something."

She rolled her eyes. "Exactly. It's crowded. Full of people I have to live around on a daily basis. So it's better I watch for flying elbows myself."

Not the hill to die on. "Whatever suits. But you could

do with dialing down the tension. Given it's crowded with, as you said, people you have to live around."

Her petite frame deflated.

"Tell me what you want from me this weekend." Never mind that he knew what she really wanted from him. And it was something he'd never be able to give.

She grimaced. "Sleeping together last month—well, it didn't exactly turn out how I expected."

"Closure was a pipe dream?"

The dim, recessed lights overhead shone in her damp eyes. *Damn.* "You could say that."

"So, like I said, tell me what you want."

"I want to *not* have this conversation in the middle of a packed, scuzzy bar, Tavish."

Fine. If waiting would make her less anxious, he'd extend her that courtesy. "No insulting the Moose, now. Pretty sure it adds to your family's bottom line more than the ski hill does."

A genuine smile, the first he'd seen on her face all day, spread across her lips. "You're probably right. Meet me for a paddle around the lake tomorrow morning. Nine, at the East Moosehorn boat ramp?"

"Done."

They managed to hold on to the bit of levity while collecting their drinks and returning to the table. But the minute they rejoined Cadie, she tensed up again.

He sighed. Her own worst enemy, his ex-wife.

She reached for her drink and popped the cherry between plump, glossy lips.

Visions of those lips wrapped around him made him hard as the goddamn table leg.

Hell. Maybe he should bow out politely, join the crowd on the dance floor. Better than being in the vicinity of

Lauren's pouty mouth. Better than wanting to kiss that pout away. "I should go give Drew his drink."

Cadie caught his forearm. "He's too busy feeling up Mackenzie to hold a drink. Stay. Chat. I'll get the next round."

Having spent their teens staring at each other, communicating without words, Tavish figured Lauren would correctly interpret the I-can't-exactly-say-no-to-your-sister look he tossed her way.

She nodded and pursed her lips around the straw of her cocktail.

And so began the longest ten minutes of Tavish's life. He managed to smile, talk with Cadie about her son and her job, tell her about Russia and Peru and his next contract—a job in Phuket starting in September. He'd been lined up to go to Nunavut in northern Canada—a follow-up to his Alaska trip—immediately after finishing his stint at WiLA, but that had fallen through.

"You're not working for the rest of the summer?" Disbelief edged Lauren's voice. "I thought you couldn't live without your job. Direct quote, in fact."

Her jab landed, blunt and heavy, on his rib cage. Some of the last words he'd spoken to her before they'd decided to separate came back to him. *Lauren, I want this marriage. Really. I've wanted you since I was fifteen and now that I have you I don't want to let you go. But I can't take pictures of Montana forever.* And could remember her reply, too. He'd just buried it deep enough that it didn't surface. Ever.

"Even I can take a break, Lauren."

"Since when?" The question hovered on a screech.

"Since I realized I needed to go somewhere without seeing it through the viewfinder of my Nikon."

Cadie's gaze shot between them, as if she was trying

to follow the conversation but knew well and good she was missing something. "Are you going to hang around here, Tavish?"

He laughed. "Yeah, no. I'll be gone the minute the happy couple gets back from their honeymoon. If I can't get another job to pass the time, I think I'll head to Australia and get some skiing in."

A shadow passed across Cadie's face and it was his turn to cringe about bringing up a subject that reminded her of her husband's death. "Right," she said in a shaky voice. "Skiing. Fun." Her attention fixed on a point across the room. She narrowed her eyes. "Good grief. Zach should not be dancing. Not even with his crutches. Excuse me."

She left, melting into the crowd on the dance floor. Tavish kept his gaze on the clusters of people dancing under the swirling lights and pulled from his beer. "Is Zach one of her rehab clients or something?" Drew's assistant had moved to town last summer, so Tavish didn't really know the guy.

"No, just a good friend. He was close to Sam." Lauren's words came out irregular, chopped with strain.

And when he looked at her, her face twitched with obvious effort to stay blank. What was she trying to hide from him? He couldn't see it having anything to do with Zach. Maybe she didn't like to see her sister upset? What had they been talking about before that…? Ben. Cadie's work. His end-of-summer travel—*Oh*. His gut hollowed.

Their stay-versus-go argument, yet again. The last time they'd hashed out their relationship, they'd ended up with their clothes strewed over Lauren's kitchen. And though he didn't expect another trip down memory lane—or being presented with an itemized list of his failings—to lead to more naked shenanigans, he didn't see the point of dwelling on their miles-apart needs.

The desire to tell her what she wanted to hear ripped through him—that he'd be happy to stay in Montana for the summer, see if they could work things out. But that smacked way too hard of his dad's broken promises. Tavish refused to lie to a woman about what he could be for her.

Offering up a cheerless smile, she said, "You look serious."

"You, too."

Her quiet laugh held a good portion of *Yeah, you think?*

"All things considered, I think we're holding it together pretty well. Being in a wedding party is a special kind of torture on a good day."

She laughed again. A sad one, but he'd take a laugh over tears.

"Really," he continued, "we should get an award for this. Fate's really rubbing our faces in it, making us watch our siblings get married." Gripping his bottle in both hands—yeah, it would warm the beer inside, but he didn't want Lauren to see him fidget, or worse, give in to the temptation to pull her into his lap and kiss her until the turned-down corners of her mouth curved up—he peered down at said siblings. Drew was an island of navy and white in the middle of a hot-pink sea.

A fast country song blasted on the speakers. Mackenzie was shaking her groove thing as best she could with seven and a half months of baby belly out in front—that had to be throwing off her center of gravity by now.

"How did you find a maternity prom dress just that ugly?" he asked Lauren.

"One of the other bridesmaids is a wunderkind with a needle. She altered it. Raised the skirt to an empire line and—" She cut herself off with a knowing look. "And you don't care."

"Not about the details, no. Wish I had my camera, though. Kenz's smile is pretty terrific picture fodder." He pulled out his phone and did his best to capture his sister's joy with his limited technology.

Mackenzie must have felt her ears burning because she looked up and wagged a no-paparazzi finger at him. The gesture turned to a clear *You and you. Get your asses on the dance floor.*

Lauren's hand landed on his knee. Her fingers dug in. "Tavish, we can't dance. The last time…"

"Yeah, I remember. You were the bride."

You were the bride.

Yup, she had been. And, once again, his strong hand gripped hers and was pulling her onto a dance floor. The energy in the club at their Vegas hotel had been similar to tonight. Her fingers dug into Tavish's shoulders as uncontrollable flashes of affixing a veil over her up-do and sliding a garter into place dominated her mind. Then, they'd only lasted ten minutes on the floor before escaping up to their room to avoid public indecency charges. Not happening tonight. Tonight was about this weekend's bride and groom. She had to make sure the night ended with no one being the wiser to veils and garters and honeymoon dances.

And with him remaining clueless about the baby. That plus sign had changed Lauren's mind—in an instant she'd known motherhood was the right choice for her. But she couldn't make that choice for Tavish. And when she'd given him an out last year, he'd taken it all too easily… God forbid he get spooked and leave before Andrew and Mackenzie had the chance to tie the knot.

The beginnings of a headache throbbed behind her eyes. Dropped her forehead to his hard chest, she inhaled the warm, woodsy scent lingering on the cotton hugging his delicious muscles. The fragrance soothed like pain medication, unraveling some of the tension pulling at her facial muscles.

He lowered his head close to her ear. "It's just one dance, Lauren. For Mackenzie's sake."

"Can't disappoint the bride."

"We should probably get used to it. Don't the best man and maid of honor have to dance at the reception?"

She tilted her chin to meet his gaze and made a face.

He matched her scrunched expression, then grabbed her hand and spun her in an awkward circle before bringing her close again. She bit her lip to hide her amusement. Tavish wasn't much of a dancer, though he tried. They'd spent most of his prom wrapped in each other.

She hadn't bothered to go to hers. He'd been in Europe on a college exchange, and she hadn't wanted to torture herself, so she'd studied for her advanced placement biology final instead.

"What are you thinking about?" he asked, voice as low as it could be given the throbbing, slow beat.

"How I aced my AP biology final."

"Huh?"

She sighed. "Prom. You missed my prom."

His hands tensed in their loose loop around her back. "Thought I apologized for that before, during and after the event itself."

"Yeah, you did."

"And I'm pretty sure you got back at me for it by dumping my ass."

"I didn't dump you because you missed my prom."

She'd dumped him because she'd known he'd miss

every other important event in their lives. Her med school aspirations and his dream of being on the cover of *National Geographic* had misaligned worse than the cock-eyed, neon beer signs adorning the scarred black walls of the Moose. There had been no point to waiting for the inevitable collapse. And their ring-exchange experiment had proved she'd been way smarter at nineteen than at twenty-nine.

Pink bled into Lauren's peripheral vision as Mackenzie sidled up, hands over her head and hips shaking. Andrew stood behind her with his hands on her waist—or lack thereof. A disgruntled wrinkle formed on Mackenzie's forehead. "Are you guys arguing again?" She shouted to be heard over the raucous beer-and-whiskey song currently entertaining the crowd.

Tavish flattened a *Who, me?* palm to his chest.

Better to let him deal with his sister. She had Andrew to handle. Her brother was eyeing her as if he finally had all the pieces of a jigsaw puzzle laid out and was about to start assembling them. She huffed out a dry laugh. No way could he guess the past she shared with Tavish.

Or the future, for that matter.

She yelled, "We're fine," at her brother and mirrored Mackenzie's arms-up, hips-boogying shuffle. Exhaustion settled in her joints, made it hard to keep her body loose and in time with the beat. If she could predict the future, maybe she could get her nerves to settle, could muster the guts to haul Tavish off the dance floor, find a quiet bench outside and be honest with him. She fought the urge to touch her stomach. She wanted the connection, but wasn't ready to broadcast the baby to the world—to Tavish.

The song's tempo picked up for the final chorus and the movement of the people around them lost the rhythm, turned a little frantic. Eyes wide, Mackenzie nestled into Andrew's tall frame.

"Come closer, sweetheart." Tavish tugged at Lauren's hand, raised an eyebrow when she glared at him.

Sweetheart? Shut up, she mouthed, glancing at Mackenzie and Andrew to make sure they hadn't heard Tavish's slip.

Before she could get a good read on their faces, an arm flailed out from the group next to them, smacking her on the side of the head. She let out a yelp and ducked.

Concern flashed across Tavish's face and he threw up a hand, shielding her from further jostling. And he must not have been anticipating the DJ leaving dead air between songs—must have lost his fricking mind, to boot—because his bellow rang clear across the bar. "Watch yourself around my wife, you prick."

Chapter Six

Colored lights imprinted on Lauren's retinas and the skin of her cheeks numbed as her brain stuttered to a halt. Her knees shook. Tavish hadn't just called her his wife in front of two hundred Sutter Creek residents, had he? He couldn't have. In front of her brother? And Mackenzie? Probably Cadie, too…

"Wife?"

"What the hell?"

Andrew and Mackenzie's shocked responses blended together, answering the question Lauren really hadn't wanted answered.

Oh, God. Her mind whirred. This called for major damage control. Maybe they could keep the news in the family for the weekend, just until the wedding was done. But splashes of pink clothing surrounded her. Fascination blazed on the other bachelorette party attendees' faces. Tavish's holler had reached their ears, all right.

All wrong, more like.

"Tavish?" Mackenzie's shrill tone stabbed Lauren between the ribs.

"I—uh—" Didn't seem like his brain was functioning any faster than Lauren's. But someone had to say something.

"Ex-wife," she offered weakly.

"As if that's better. Why did we not know?" Mackenzie let out a loud curse and looked like she couldn't decide who best deserved her stabby glare. "And you had to announce this *now*? Stellar timing."

"Mackenzie—" Tavish started.

She held up a hand. "No. No excuses. I'm going home." Pushing her way off the dance floor, she was out the door with Andrew on her heels before Lauren could get her legs to move.

Her feet were stuck to the floor, muscles immobile from shame. Heart hammering hard enough it threatened to break a rib, she sent her big-mouthed ex-husband a disbelieving glare. *"Tavish."*

"What's going on?" Cadie materialized at Lauren's side. "Why did Mackenzie leave? And did you just say 'wife'?"

"Ex-wife," she repeated, snapping out the word. "I'm sure Tavish would love to explain given he's the one who announced it to the entire bar."

Anger darkened Cadie's eyes. "Well, someone had better fill me in."

Tavish's hand landed on Lauren's shoulder. "Lauren, I'm sorry, I—"

"Sorry? You're *sorry*? Too late!" Snatching the martini glass from Cadie's hand, she sloshed the blue drink into Tavish's face.

Eyes closed, he slowly ran his tongue over his lips—

oh, how dare he look smoking hot after what he did tonight—and wiped the sleeve of his no-longer-white dress shirt over his cheeks. "Seriously?"

Regret immediately crawled into her stomach. So much for keeping a low profile. "I owe you a drink, Cadie."

"No, you owe me an explanation! You were *married*?"

"Yeah, well—"

"And you're not now?"

"No, we—"

A single sob interrupted Lauren's attempt to explain. Cadie's shoulders jerked and her chest visibly shuddered.

Lauren would have been able to handle anger or any of its by-products. But the tears streaking down Cadie's blotched face made the backs of Lauren's eyes sting. She followed her sister to their table. She sensed Tavish close behind but couldn't bring herself to look at him. Anger churned through her belly. At him, yeah. But more at herself.

"Cadie, I should have told you. But you had Sam's death to deal with, and then Ben arrived, and it never seemed important."

Her sister's jaw dropped. "You don't think you're important to me?"

"Of course I do, I just didn't think—"

"You're more than my sister, Laur. You're my best friend. Or I thought you were. But friends don't lie to each other, and you did *this morning*. Said you weren't involved."

She wasn't going to insult her sister by pulling out a "Technically, we're not involved anymore." She'd be connected to Tavish for the rest of her life, though in a far different way than they'd hoped for when they'd promised each other a life of love and respect. Forever in the marriage sense had lasted all of twelve days. Forever in the parenting sense would be starting in around mid-February, give or take.

She should just blurt that out, too. A cherry on tonight's fricking drama cake.

But no. There was a sacredness to telling a man he was going to be a father. No matter her ire, she wouldn't take away what would hopefully be a poignant moment for him.

Unless he deserts you again...

She shoved the thought from her mind. She'd worry about that after the wedding. First, she had to fix things with her sister. Mackenzie and Andrew, too. She sent Cadie a pleading look. "You have enough to worry about without taking on my problems."

"I'm not fragile. I would have been there for you, just like you have for me." Cadie started to back up.

"I know. I screwed up—"

"Yeah, you did. I naively thought I meant as much to you, that you'd rely on me if you needed me. Obviously not. Relationships need to go two ways, Lauren. It can't just be you giving all the time." Cadie grabbed her jacket from the booth. "I need to make sure Mackenzie's okay."

Lauren sucked in a breath as her sister spun and retreated. With each of Cadie's steps, all Lauren's attempts to shore up her family slowly drained away. Her closeness with her sister, gone. And as soon as her dad found out, he'd probably react the same as Cadie. Protecting her family from more pain—the purpose of having kept the secret—was supposed to have helped them stay together, not push them apart.

Tavish held a clean dishcloth under the faucet in Mackenzie and Drew's kitchen. Cleaning the blue cocktail off his face was child's play compared to cleaning up the mess he'd made by letting his temper get the best of him. He'd spent a good hour trying to convince his sister that the secret coming to light actually meant he and Lauren *wouldn't* be sniping at each other for the rest of the weekend. A bald-faced lie, obviously—thirty seconds after Cadie had left the bar, Lauren had stormed out, still looking like she'd have preferred to crack a beer bottle over his head instead of throwing that drink in his face. But the dishonesty was necessary to get Mackenzie to believe that tomorrow's rehearsal and Saturday's wedding would go off without a hitch.

Footsteps on the tiled kitchen floor announced Drew's return from tucking Mackenzie in. Arms crossed over his chest, he hitched a hip on the counter and fixed an impressive serious-ski-patroller look on his face. "When I suggested we start the weekend off with a bang, that's not what I had in mind."

Tavish flinched. He'd earned the thinly veiled disgust. Keeping his marriage a secret had been easy enough to do when he never saw Lauren. A change in proximity shouldn't have altered the parameters *that* much. "I don't even know where to start."

"Start by telling me Lauren got home safe tonight."

Damn it, he couldn't even guarantee that. Wringing out the cloth, he bought himself a few seconds by hanging it over the kitchen faucet and ambling over to one of the bar stools tucked under the kitchen counter. He spun the stool around, straddled it and rested his arms on the wooden back. "She took off before I could talk to her."

Drew yanked his phone from his pocket and typed out a rapid message. "And Vegas, Fitz? How did you get married without me noticing? I mean, we were drunk a good chunk of the time, but not *that* drunk."

No, but on what should have been their last morning, Tavish had left Drew sawing logs in their hotel room to meet Lauren for brunch.

The minute she had smiled with her lips pursed around the rim of her coffee cup, Tavish had known in every particle of his being that he wanted to stare at that smile over the breakfast table for the rest of his life. They hadn't dated for a decade. But his heart had clung to her, no matter how far he'd traveled.

"Marry me, Pixie," he'd blurted.

"That's Dr. Pixie to you," she'd joked. All the gold had faded from her eyes, leaving them a deep, shocked green. "You're serious. Tav. *Oh.*"

He'd counted. *One. Two. Three. Four.*

On *five*, she'd crawled onto his lap right in the middle of the hotel restaurant. Her hungry, hands-to-the-face kiss had said "yes" for her.

"Tonight?" he'd asked.

She'd nodded, then disappeared for the rest of the day. And when he'd seen her in the chapel... Holy hell. Straight hair curled into submission and piled on her head. Sky-high stilettos that hadn't brought her close to his height, though he'd grinned at the effort. And her dress. That scrap of silk still taunted him in his dreams.

As did their promises. *For richer, for poorer, to have and to hold.*

And her fingers had snapped in his face.

Wait, that's not right.

Fingers *were* snapping in his face. Drew's.

"Dude, what?" Blood pounded in his head. He filled a glass of water and drained half of it.

"Lost you for a minute. Focus. You. My sister. Married."

"Yeah. You left. We didn't. We'd intended to come

home from our honeymoon and make the announcement in person. But then we got the call about your grandparents' car accident. After that, everyone was grieving." She'd floored him with an ultimatum—stay in town or file for divorce—right after the funeral. "Seemed easier to keep it between the two of us."

Drew's brow knitted. "So it was just a random Vegas thing?"

"No. No way. We honestly thought we could make a go of it. But neither of us wanted a part-time marriage, with me gone most of the year."

"How did you not think of that beforehand?"

Being condescended to like a kindergarten student was the opposite of awesome, but Drew deserved answers. Finally releasing the valve on his secrets was a welcome relief, too.

"We'd agreed to switch up who was working at any given time. Me taking contracts in between her working stints in overseas areas." Tavish shook his head. "When your grandparents died, she backpedaled from buying plane tickets and researching humanitarian missions to calling Frank Martin about committing to a future partnership. I told her I couldn't give up my job. And she gave her ring back."

Tavish rubbed that same ring, twisted and disguised as one of the links on his bracelet. Entwined with his own band. A constant reminder he couldn't be trusted with someone else's heart.

Drew's gaze flattened. "You both should have compromised. Especially you. Marriage surpasses everything."

Easy for Drew to say. Tavish agreed that most of the time, marriage ranked above all else. But he didn't believe it was right for either him or Lauren to change the utter fabric of their personalities for the sake of staying together. "With my assignments, I can't settle in one place."

The other man drummed his fingers on the table. "Selfish."

"Documenting refugee crises is selfish?"

"It is if you're putting your job before my sister."

Tavish took a breath. He rubbed at his breastbone. *No. Our split was for the best.* As a kid, he'd lain awake for too many nights listening to his mother sobbing in the kitchen after one of his father's few-and-far-between phone calls. He had loved Lauren too much to want to subject her to an equally miserable marriage.

Had loved. Right. Try "still loved."

And probably always would.

Crack. Plop.
Thwoop. Crack.
Plop.

Oh, *no, no, no.* Lauren hated waking up to the sounds of club hitting ball, had purposely not bought a house near the golf course to avoid the torture. She'd cursed her childhood-bedroom view of the eighth tee of the Sutter Creek Golf Club many a time as a teenager. Unless she'd fallen asleep at her dad's…

Rolling over, she blinked. Nope, the sunlight streaming in through the skylight placed her firmly in her lake-side house.

And threatened to split her head. How the hell did she feel hungover without having had anything to drink? Oh, wait. A scant two hours of sleep would do it.

And the neighbor currently preventing her from sleeping away last night's humiliation was lucky she was the one person in Montana who didn't own a hunting rifle.

Thwoop. Crack.

Dragging herself over to her open window—it sounded like she was almost on top of the noise—she spotted the perpetrator.

Tavish oozed a weekend-sexy "Exercise is nice and all, but I'm better made for putting down this driver and sliding between your sheets" aura. He stood on the middle level of her tiered deck with a driver grasped in both hands. His gray athletic shorts sat low on his hips, right below that delectable, lick-worthy ridge of muscle that arrowed toward his groin. An ancient University of Montana ball cap sat backward over his tawny hair. His T-shirt hung out of the back of his waistband. With each swing the balls easily hit the middle of the six-hundred-yard-wide lake.

Squinting against the bright sunshine and the resulting jab to her retinas, she didn't call the knee-jerk "You're breaking the law, idiot!" out the open window, instead taking a moment to lean on the sill and stare at the view. He'd woken her up, so it was only fair she steal the opportunity to appreciate that admirable expanse of sexy torso. His tattoo rippled as he aimed and knocked a ball far enough into Moosehorn Lake to make a pro green.

Her stomach flipped, ending the pleasure.

Morning sickness? Fury?

Both.

At least fifty percent of her wanted him to follow his golf balls to the murky lake bottom and not return.

The other half was going to relish looking at him. A blessed distraction from the mammoth task of convincing her family to forgive her. And as much as Tavish's announcement had been the catalyst for last night's fiasco, she was at fault. She'd lied by omission to protect her family, not to hurt them. Talk about backfiring. Why hadn't she been honest? Not the day after her grandparents' funeral, but some point in the past year. At least then she would have been able to control the way they found out.

After brushing her teeth and scrounging a pregnancy-safe painkiller from her bathroom cabinet, she pulled sweatpants and a dilapidated Colorado Avalanche T-shirt from her closet and headed out to confront Tavish. He'd make an excellent patsy on whom to pawn her self-loathing.

She pulled her sliding door open. The metallic scrape made her head pound with fresh enthusiasm. She held her hand against her forehead to combat the dizziness.

Tavish turned, but stayed on the deck a level below her, arms loose at his sides, golf club in his right hand. Dropping the driver to the planking, he quickly pulled his shirt out of his shorts and over his head.

The sun made her orbital bones ache. The decking chilled her bare feet. And the look of utter misery on Tavish's face dulled the temptation to project any self-directed anger toward him.

Why, why, why did she become such a sucker whenever undiluted emotion crossed the absurdly beautiful planes of his face? Only one way to protect herself from her own weakness—evasion.

"Shh," she pleaded. "Pretty sure my headache just got classified as category five."

"Sorry, sweetheart." His lips twisted in regret. He picked his club back up and spun it like a top, catching the shaft before it could clatter to the deck. "Did you drink last night?"

"No."

"So why the headache?"

She winced at the stiffness in her neck as she sat on

the top of the three-stair set between decks and curled her bare toes around the middle step. "Barely slept."

"That why you bailed on me for our morning paddle?"

"Oh, crap…" She screwed up her face in apology. "Our plans slipped my mind when the night got eventful."

The guilty flush in his cheeks deepened from pink to crimson. "If I could rewind, I would, Laur."

"I know." She tried to dig out a sympathetic expression. Wasn't sure if she managed one, but he smiled back, at least. "This is going to affect you as much as it does me. It's too bad…" The first positive thought of the day struck, warmed her. "No. It was bound to come out at some point. I guess now was better than five, ten years in the future. Our families would have been even angrier had we kept the secret longer. So why not yesterday?"

Tavish's mouth gaped for a few seconds. "Oh, the wedding. Us working together. Take your pick."

"Good points. And don't get me wrong—I'm upset. My sister is beyond pissed at me. A good chunk of the town witnessed the likely candidate for the most embarrassing moment of my life. But at the same time, I feel—" she surprised herself with the word that came to mind "—free."

Tavish palmed the top of his frayed-around-the-edges maroon ball cap. "Free? How?"

"My slate's clean. No more lies. No more secrets." Her conscience poked at her. Okay, one. Maybe it was wrong to wait, even for two more days… "So…my deck. Golfing. Interesting—and illegal—choice."

His fist pulsed a few times around the grip of his club. "When you didn't show up for our paddle, I figured you were avoiding me. I needed to be able to pretend I was here for some other reason than to beg your forgiveness."

Lauren's mouth turned sandy. "Beg?"

"On figurative knees." He shifted his feet. "Real ones, if it'll make the difference."

A replay of what Tavish had done to her the last time he'd been in front of her on his knees cut through the throbbing in her head. Heat blasted her cheeks. "Not necessary. I believe you."

"Huh. I wasn't expecting you to be so agreeable."

"I've spent a lot of time—" she sighed "—the whole year, really, feeling sorry for myself, feeling you gave up on me. I assumed my family would do the same if they learned the truth. And because of my dishonesty, well, I wouldn't blame them if they did."

He opened his mouth, protest written in his eyes.

She held up a hand. "But feeling sorry for myself isn't going to fix anything. I need to earn their forgiveness. Try to put things back to normal so that Andrew and Mackenzie can have a stellar wedding."

He cocked an eyebrow, too playful for comfort. "You sure you don't want me to beg?"

She bit her lip. "Nothing good happens when you beg me for things, Tavish."

"Yeah?" He reached forward with the driver, dragged the cool metal head along the top of her bare foot.

"Yeah. It usually ends up with me losing my dignity."

"Your clothes, maybe. But not your dignity."

His sensual tone dragged along her skin, delved into the needy parts of her core. A strangled gurgle escaped her. "Okay, if I'm going to forgive you and we're going to make sense of this, that has to stop. No innuendos, no remembering the past, no pretending anything about our relationship worked. You're leaving."

He gave a nod, blanked the hints of sexual promise from his face. "That is what I do."

"I'm staying." She had to adhere to that decision more than ever. Her child—their child—would need stability.

"That is what you do." He spoke church-quiet. Church-serious.

"And because we both have to live with whatever happens here—" she waved a finger back and forth between her chest and Tavish's "—we need to recognize there's no way we can go back to any part of what we had."

"Oh, I recognize that but good." His sardonic tone spread to his eyes, darkening the violet to thunderstorm gray. The identical shade his irises turned post-sex.

Her brain surged with discomfiting flashes of sneaking kisses down hidden trails the summer he'd graduated, of lounging in their king-sized honeymoon bed, of the weight of her wedding ring on her finger.

She rubbed her temples for a few seconds, then pressed her fingers to her eyelids, but failed to clear her head.

He stared at her, spun his golf club again. "Now what?"

"Now I wait four hours until I can take another Tylenol."

The sound of a vial of pills being shaken prompted her to open her eyes.

Tavish held out a travel-size container of generic acetaminophen.

She shook her head. "I've already had my limit. Uh, you always carry around painkillers?"

"No. Your brother and I had a long talk last night, after which I reacquainted myself with Johnnie Walker."

"We make quite the pair."

"Yeah, we do." Tavish's eyes shone just enough to betray his vulnerability.

Unbearable. She threw up her hands. "What did I just say?"

"You said no more lies."

Her headache stopped her from shaking her head. "No, I said we can't go back."

"Sure. Doesn't mean I don't wish we could."

"Don't wish. *Don't.*" She'd wasted a heap of good wishes on Tavish Fitzgerald. Birthday candles. The first star to appear on countless clear summer evenings. Coins thrown backward over her shoulder into the grizzly-bear-shaped fountain in the town square.

Wishes only resulted in a lighter change purse and a whole lot of shame. She'd almost given up her dream of the clinic for him. She'd convinced herself that her mother would have been okay with the change in plans for the sake of Lauren finding love with the man she'd wanted almost as long as she'd wanted to be a doctor. She could at least thank Tavish for his timing. At least he'd showed his true inability-to-stick colors before she'd burned bridges with Frank Martin.

He let his club clatter to the ground and shoved his hands into his pockets. "You can't tell me you never wonder, Lauren."

"No, I can't." Pulse racing, she twisted her hands. She didn't need to wonder. She knew. Knew his lips could coax a moan from her mouth and his hands could drive her body into a frenzy. The craving to let him swirled in her belly.

Ignore it, ignore it.

But how?

With a blur of limbs and lips and lust, Lauren stood and pressed herself into him, trying to kiss him out of her system. She melted into his magnetic heat. And he wasn't resisting. His lips caressed hers with a fervent thirst. His fingers grasped her hips with enough force to leave marks.

Her hands roamed his back. Took in the texture of cotton and tight muscle. Creeping her fingers up the warm skin of his neck, she wove them into the short waves at his nape, knocking off his ball cap.

She stretched onto her toes and he held her secure. Physically secure, anyway. Emotionally, she was slipping from her stable footing.

His fingers slid under the elastic of her sweats, teased her lower back at the edge of her panties.

Common sense, Lauren. Do not set yourself up for another broken heart.

She tore her reluctant-to-be-torn-away lips from his and backed up. What was she thinking? If they were going to have any chance at a functioning coparent relationship, she needed to keep her hands to herself.

And more than that, she needed to tell him. For him to understand just how stupid it would be for them to have sex again, he needed to know all the variables.

"Tavish..." She swallowed.

"Yeah?" He smiled, a feral flash of straight white teeth. His chest rose and fell rapidly.

Taking a step backward, she settled on a stair edge. "Come sit for a second."

His face screwed up in confusion. "Huh?"

Nausea panged in her stomach. *Ack, not now.* "I need to tell you something."

"Okay..." He eased down next to her on the stair and reached for her knee, but dropped his hand to his side before making contact.

She swallowed the saliva flooding her mouth. "I— Oh, crap." Running for the deck railing, she hung over the edge and heaved what little was left of her dinner from last night into the huckleberry and Oregon grape plants covering the ground below.

"You sure you didn't drink last night?" Tavish was at her side in a second, gripping her shoulders with unyielding hands as she crossed her arms on the railing and buried her face in her elbow.

"Positive. I can't drink. I'm pregnant."

Chapter Seven

"That's a lot of blue lines," Tavish croaked as he took in the four positive pregnancy tests arranged into a military-precise row on Lauren's bathroom vanity. She'd been kind, humoring him by running to the drugstore to pick up the tests. He'd believed her when she'd told him. But at the same time, he'd wanted to see the proof.

Hello, proof.

His knees wobbled and he sat down on the edge of the fancy-ass marble bathtub before he completely humiliated himself by collapsing on the floor. The grout pattern between the shiny, white tiles swam in his vision as he clenched the side of the tub and blinked. Cold seeped into his palms and a chill spread through his limbs. He shivered and drew in a too-shallow breath.

Lauren plunked down next to him and held out a small, plastic trash can. "Just in case."

The numbness gripping his body shattered. One loud

ha turned into two and then a cascade of near manic laughter.

And she let him have his moment to completely lose it. She set a gentle palm on his back, murmured, "I know," but left it at that.

He managed to catch himself before his harsh guffaws turned into sobs. He hadn't cried in years. Decades. But if he let down a child like his father let down their family? Son of a bitch, his tear ducts stung. "How did the condom break without us knowing it?"

"Who knows? Microscopic tear? They're not fail-safe."

He let out an ear-blistering curse.

"Look," she murmured, "you don't have to decide anything today. I know neither of us was sure about having kids before…"

"Irrelevant now."

"No, it's not. No one's forcing me to have this baby—I know my options. But I have the resources to be a single parent. And we can figure out how much or how little you are going to be involved—"

"You're not going to be a single parent, Lauren. I watched my mom burn the candle at both ends and sacrifice too damn much to *ever* let you go through the same. I'm going to be involved."

She startled and her hand moved to his shoulder in what seemed like an attempt to steady herself.

The ferocity of his vow surprised him, too. Did he believe he had it in him to be a reliable father? No. For the sake of the child—his child, their child—cutting and running might be best. Deserting her, though, deserting a baby… Acid bit his throat and he almost had to take her up on the offer of the garbage can to puke in.

Swallowing, he let out a dry laugh. "And here I thought screwing up yesterday was as eventful as it could get."

Her mouth quirked. "This news we should definitely keep to ourselves. We have time, Tav. Let's settle in to this a bit before we commit to anything."

He recognized her words for what they were—an out. Checks and balances to make sure they didn't race head-long into an arrangement that crashed and burned like their marriage had. And he respected her caution.

Had he earned her doubt? Hell, yeah. Did he wish it could be different? Yeah, just as much as—no, more than—he had for the last year when it came to their failed marriage.

"Look, I have an appointment to get to. And we both have the rehearsal to deal with." She put a hand to her stomach, that ubiquitous pregnant-woman gesture he'd never before felt connected to. But now... His palm grew restless with the urge to slide over her hand. He resisted temptation.

"I guess I'll see you later, then," he said.

"It's probably best." Her face, pale since she'd been sick on the balcony, shifted into a forced smile.

And as he strode from the room he cursed how he always managed to be the one leaving, always managed to prove himself his father's son.

A few minutes later he sat in his SUV, frozen with his hands on the steering wheel. He needed to get into town, to go to Mackenzie's and apologize again. But if he went to talk to his sister without decompressing some, she'd sniff out that something was wrong.

No, wrong wasn't the word. But right didn't fit, either. He shook his head. He needed time to think.

We have time, Tav.

Huh. He hadn't noticed it at the time, but Lauren had

shortened his name. For the first time in a year, to his memory. Warmth eased some of the chill from his insides. He didn't like admitting how good her familiarity made him feel. How desperate he was for scraps of what they'd had.

Yet another thing to contemplate. Turning the key in the ignition, his internal autopilot kicked in, pointing the car away from town. Driving down a gravel road, he cranked his stereo, let some old-school Bruce Springsteen force out thoughts of his wife. *Pregnant wife. Ex. Ex-wife. Either way, though, pregnant.*

He parked in a turnout five hundred yards from his thinking spot. Back in high school he'd found a nook of sandy riverbank that had become his refuge when he was yearning to escape but couldn't. He'd taken his first award-winning picture at sixteen there, had figured out photography was his ticket out of Sutter Creek.

Pulling his sketch pad and beat-up wooden pencil case—filled to bursting with charcoals, chalk pastels and graphite and watercolor pencils—from under the passenger seat, he headed for the grass-lined trail. He trudged down the uneven path and reached the little clearing, a patch of sand just big enough for two people to sit with their feet in the water. He'd come here with Lauren. Would he be coming here with their kid in a few years? Before filing for divorce, she'd made it very clear she wouldn't want a half-time husband. But he wanted some sort of regular visitation. What that would look like, well, they'd have to work on that.

Sighing, he kicked at the sand with a toe. The river ran a muted, glacial jade, opaque in the center fading to clear green on the edges. The scent of baking pines and sweet grass hovered between cloying and refreshing as it eddied in the breeze. Settling against his log, Tavish took off his sandals. He breathed in Montana wilderness and put pencil to paper. He could have easily taken a series of stunning photos to capture nature's majesty. But his work was commercial. Sketching was personal, something he did for himself. And this place mattered enough that he'd had it inked on his side last winter.

He set about recreating what he'd captured in a photograph back at sixteen. Juniper-green pencil blended into walnut brown and warm gray. Smudging his strokes with a fingertip and water, he managed a passable interpretation of the river rushing over a rock a few feet away from his submerged heels. He stared at his creation. Knew that color.

Remembered making the comparison to Lauren's eyes the last time he'd been here with her.

Right after the funeral, she'd been frantic. He'd calmed her down with words and hands and pleasure. If only they'd stopped there. The minute they'd started talking, she'd shocked him with her sudden change from wanting to travel the world with him to never wanting to go five miles past home again. She needed to be with her family, needed to follow through on the clinic. And when he'd pointed out that those desires might fade as she worked through her grief for her grandparents, she'd vowed she'd never change her mind.

Somehow, that train wreck of a day hadn't tainted this place for good.

He turned and smoothed the page. Pencils flew. Green to brown again, then cream and medium flesh tone for skin, the occasional raw sienna freckle, a mix of ocher and cadmium yellows for hair… Maybe the act of physically putting Lauren on paper would free his mind.

It certainly couldn't make him want her more. He was

already teetering precariously on the edge of that cliff again.

And he hated how much it would hurt when he landed. Because he wouldn't be landing anywhere good. This pregnancy had struck any more casual sex between them right off the table.

A baby was the one tie they couldn't undo. A little being that might have eyes as hazel as Lauren's, or maybe the shock of blond curls he'd had as a kid...

Sketching and smudging, he lost track of time. His feet went numb from being in the rushing water.

A vibration in his pocket jarred him from his artistic zone. He checked his cell display. Mackenzie. *Crap.*

He decided to head her off at the proverbial pass. "Hey, Kenz. Sorry, I was going to come by this morning, but I got caught up—"

"With your tuxedo fitting?" she cut in.

Tuxedo fitting. Double crap. "What time is it?"

"Noon." She sounded singularly unimpressed. "You missed your appointment."

"I— No. I went over to talk to Lauren and then had... other stuff that came up. I'll go do it right now." He snapped his sketch pad shut and squeezed his phone between his shoulder and his ear to allow him both hands to pack up his pencil case and do up the toggles on his sandals.

"Okay. I have my final appointment in a few minutes, too. Come see me when you're done with yours. Penance, big brother. You owe me."

"I do." He started jogging down the trail. "Give me fifteen minutes."

A few winding roads and one stoplight later, he was back in Sutter Creek and in Dreamy & Dapper's parking lot.

After confirming that he wasn't a total moron and the measurements he'd emailed the store were indeed correct, he readjusted his ball cap on his head and strolled to the women's side of the store. By the glare the sales associate directed at his feet, he guessed there was some rule about wearing shoes around the overpriced, overspangled merchandise, so he slid out of his Keens and padded over to a plush pink chair. Sat among the sparkly stilettos and the poufy gowns and the pervasive memory of standing up at the altar with Lauren, her curves enhanced by a fussy little dress. *Penance, indeed.* He groaned inwardly and shoved the vision away, but the general surroundings of white and frill didn't give him much of a reprieve.

"Hey." Lauren's quiet voice broke into his thoughts, saving him from certain death by overexposure to taffeta. She stood a few feet away from him, wearing what had to be her maid-of-honor dress. The sweep of turquoise silk nipped and tucked at all the right places, highlighting all his favorite parts of her petite frame. His mouth went dry. "Hey. You look…"

"Ill? I've been sick three more times this morning."

She did still look pale. And he hadn't even asked her how she was feeling. He was such an ass. "Try incredible."

A tiny smile tugged at one side of her mouth. "Didn't expect to see you here."

"I—"

"Tav! You're here." His sister rushed into the room. Well, rushed as much as she was able, given she was waddling more than walking these days.

He stood and tried to look like he was enjoying himself.

"You're so forgiven for having forgotten your appointment." Mackenzie gave him a quick kiss on his cheek, sent him a look that they'd talk later and headed for the back of the store.

White. Frills. And *alone with my ex-wife.* A few choice curses rattled around in his head in time with the lingering Johnnie Walker throb. He rubbed his eyes.

Lauren looked from his decade-old hat to the ratty Yale T-shirt he'd put on this morning when he thought they were going kayaking. "Decided not to dress up for the occasion?"

"I haven't been back to the apartment. I went out to the river—" He cut himself off. The admission seemed too intimate.

"Figured you would," she said in a low voice.

And then all the focus shifted to Mackenzie as she emerged from the dressing room. Tavish stood back, separated from the oohs and aahs and tears. Tomorrow was going to be a cryfest if this was the reaction everyone had to a swath of white fabric.

He smiled at his sister, who looked like a chic Roman fertility goddess. "You look beautiful, Kenz."

"Thanks." His sister glowed—with love, with pleasure, with the flush of motherhood.

A notion of Lauren, belly all big with his baby, cheeks pink with that same glow, popped into his head.

Um, brain? Give me a break, here. That's a ways off yet.

Though not all that far off. Time would pass. Lauren's stomach, currently flat and taut under her fancy dress, would soon curve out, no doubt making her sexier than she already was. And then they'd feel precious kicks. And she'd complain about looking like a house and would demand ice cream…

And unless he made some major changes, he'd miss all that magic.

Damn it.

* * *

Lauren didn't know what to expect from the rehearsal dinner beyond the obvious: Tavish and Mackenzie's mom, Gwen, had gone to great expense to host an upscale affair. Crystal and linens fancy enough for an actual wedding graced the round tables on the stone patio.

Shaking her head, trying to prevent her spiky slingback heels from sinking into the lawn, she knew tomorrow's mountaintop ceremony and casual cocktail party in the midstation lounge would suit her brother and his fiancée far more than tonight's swanky atmosphere. But if Mackenzie was okay with the country-clubbish feel of the yard, Lauren wouldn't make a fuss about how ridiculous it was to host a party that didn't suit the honorees. She had enough to worry about having to pretend she wasn't getting the silent treatment from the other bridesmaid. Not to mention having the best man watch her like he couldn't decide whether to wrap her in protective bubble wrap or book a flight to Tasmania. But the rehearsal had gone off without a hitch, so she'd count that as a win. Apparently no one had noticed the family drama simmering under the surface. Or if they had, they hadn't mentioned it.

And they'd better keep on not mentioning it. It sucked enough that her sister wasn't talking to her on a weekend that should have been about having a wonderful time as a family. She didn't need their second cousins from New England questioning why Cadie wouldn't look her in the face. Didn't want to explain herself one more time.

Telling her dad this morning about the divorce had been plenty. He didn't seem to be as angry as Cadie. He'd been more quiet than anything, agreeing the wedding was the priority. That had all been over the phone, though, and she wanted to confirm his forgiveness in person. She spotted him over by the linen-bedecked bar and headed his way. She felt a little calmer when she was able to wrap her arms around him and rest her cheek on his summer suit jacket. "Hi, Dad."

"Just the girl I wanted to see." He took her under his left arm and accepted a drink on the rocks from the bartender with his right. "Need a drink?"

The offer caught her off-kilter. She'd been so busy worrying about Tavish that she hadn't come up with a good excuse not to be drinking. When she'd filled her dad in about the divorce, she'd kept silent about the baby. Nor did she feel guilty about that secrecy like she had with her marriage. The pregnancy was something for her and Tavish to coddle for a while before telling anyone else. But if she wasn't careful, her not having any alcohol would get noticed.

"I'm going to hold off until dinner, I think," she explained to her dad before addressing the bartender. "Could you make me a virgin mojito?"

The bartender nodded and took out a martini shaker.

She turned her attention back to her dad. With his mirrored sunglasses stuck in his hair and his good-humored grin, he looked more ski instructor than resort owner. His years of hard work showed in the sprinkling of gray in his brown-black hair, but the crinkle lines in his forehead were from smiling, not stress. Edward Dawson lived for his family, not his company. She wanted to follow in his footsteps in that. Lucky that her family and her job were intricately woven.

A niggle of doubt teased her consciousness at the word *lucky*. She pushed it aside and returned her dad's smile.

"You look like you got some sun, Cookie. About time."

"After my vacation, my clinic hours won't be so crazy." She hoped. She'd have to talk to Frank sooner rather than later about her workload once the baby arrived.

"So you got your paperwork in?"

Lauren flashed to the stack of papers still on her table, still being ignored. "I—I will." She bit her lip. Should she tell her dad about the almost panic attacks she'd been having when she tried to scribble her signature on her contract? About the way her heart lunged into her throat whenever she pictured her name inked on the line?

"You know," her father's mouth tightened, "you don't have to sign on with the clinic. Any time I've brought it up lately, you've ended up with a frown on your face."

She closed her eyes for a few seconds. *Honesty. I said honesty.* "I…"

"You…?" he prodded.

Medicine doesn't… She stopped the gut-churning thought from finishing, took the mocktail the bartender held out and sipped away her conscience. "I'm happy, Dad. I'm going to deliver the agreement to Frank on my first day back from holidays. But I'm glad I took the time to ensure it's the right decision."

"Of course it's the right decision. You've been aiming to work in Sutter Creek since you were in high school. And your sister needs you here. As do I."

"I know." And a clinic partnership met every vocational goal she'd set. The Dawson name deserved to be on a plaque on one of the doors at the clinic again. So her trouble committing made no sense. Unless it meant… *No.*

"Your mom would be so proud of you, following in her footsteps." He laid a broad hand on the side of her head, stroked her hair. "She was a firecracker, right up to her last day. So are you."

Obligation pressed down on her chest. He had to bring out the big guns, didn't he? She wanted to be like her mom. And she didn't need the reminder that she'd been away on a stupid trip to summer camp when her mother had died of unexpected complications after a routine tumorectomy. *Stop it, Lauren*. She tried to inhale some courage. "I won't let either of you down. I've done that enough already this week."

With a slight eyebrow lift, he said, "I thought we were going to leave that alone for now."

"I still feel awful," she murmured.

"Look, I love Tavish like a son, but you'd make each other miserable. You fixed your mistake. That's what matters."

"Thanks for understanding." And for reminding her why she needed to stop scanning the property for a certain pair of violet-blue eyes.

He released her from his embrace and pressed at his sternum.

Worry shot up her spine. Hands on breastbones were rarely good signs. "You okay, Dad?"

"Eh, just reflux. Frank's got me on acid reducers."

She relaxed a tad at that admission, but not entirely. "Da-*ad*. Small symptoms can mask big problems."

"No nagging, Cookie. I'm exercising, eating right." He glanced to the side, eyes darting everywhere but her face. "Crud, I just remembered. The Creekside catering manager needed something confirmed with Mackenzie, and asked me to pass on the message. Excuse me for a bit."

He gave her one last squeeze and walked over to where her brother leaned up against the gazebo, snuggling with Mackenzie. The couple was deep in conversation with crutches-bound Zach Cardenas.

Had Lauren been in the market for a retired Olympian with rumpled hair and a cocky grin, she might have been interested in Zach. She had dated in the past year. Sutter Creek was full of eligible men during ski season, and Zach was single, well-employed, charming. But Lauren had already tested the rumpled, cockily grinning waters, and found them to be life-threatening. And Zach's green irises didn't merit a second look compared to the purple-blue light show of Tavish's eyes. A light show walking toward her right now. *Crap.*

She pivoted ninety degrees, doing her best lawn-ornament impression and poking at the mint in her drink with the straw. Had he noticed her noticing him?

She watched him from the corner of her eye. The linen-and-twinkle-light atmosphere didn't suit him any more than it did Mackenzie and Andrew. He'd put on a pleated tuxedo shirt, probably to avoid confrontation with his mother, but the top two buttons were undone and his French cuffs were open and rolled up his muscular forearms. His jeans, faded in all the right places—all the places Lauren wanted to reacquaint herself with—completed the picture of a man so comfortable in his own skin that he'd wear leather flip-flops to a fancy party and look spectacularly hot doing it. She couldn't have been more opposite from him if she'd tried. Her own feet pinched in her heels, but being maid-of-honor at a glitzy rehearsal dinner required stilettos.

From halfway across the lawn, each step he took echoed low in her belly, pulsing aches of needy curiosity. Adjusting the flared skirt of her dress, she gave in to temptation and eyed the soft, blue-white denim covering his strong thighs.

He came to a halt six inches too close to her, close enough to feel the heat of his body. If he wanted to, he could lean in and kiss her. He wouldn't, especially not in public. And she shouldn't have been disappointed by that. But she was.

Physical intimacy was so far off the table now that they were going to be parents. But an undeniable magnetic want pulled them together. Arousal tugged between her thighs. The instinct to fit her body against his tempted rather than screaming *Danger.*

You do not want that. You can't.

"People watching?" he asked, turning to face the same direction as her.

"Um, Cadie and Ben." She pointed across the lawn, to where her sister, both hands holding Ben's, bounced the baby on his chubby legs. The pair crept along. Cadie looked to be showing off for Zach, who sat on the grass. Zach had been Cadie's husband's closest friend. But by the look on Zach's face, he didn't think of her like a guy did his buddy's widow. *Hmm. Must ask Cadie about that.* If Cadie ever started talking to her again.

She sipped at her drink and racked her brain for something to fill the silence. No small talk came to mind. Only massive, life-changing topics. The baby. Her uncertainty about her job. Wanting him back in her bed. Wishing they could find a way to be in each other's lives.

To create a life together.

Though I guess we already did that...

Glancing at him, she started at his wide eyes and pale skin. "Uh, why the shell shock?"

"Ben looks like you." His words came out jagged, like he had scar tissue in his throat.

"Kind of. Except for his eyes." Her nephew's cornflower-blue irises were all Cadie. Other than that, Tavish had a point. Ben had Lauren's blond hair, different from his dark-haired mother.

"I wonder if... I mean, our, uh... Well, she or he might—"

"Yeah," she said quietly. And unless Tavish did a massive lifestyle about-face, he wouldn't be around to see the miracle of watching a child grow. He'd miss seeing fragments of his own expressions flashed back at him. God, she couldn't imagine choosing that. Preferring instability and floating on the wind over providing a firm foundation for a child.

Tavish put a hand on her lower back and rubbed tiny circles with his fingertips.

The painful truth of his choices didn't take away the pleasure of his touch. The protective, masculine, guide-her-around-the-floor weight that made her so damn hot. She filled her lungs, tried to control the hurricane whipping along her limbs. "I remember watching you teach ski school. You were great with kids."

"Sure. But growing up, it didn't matter how many times my dad would tell me he loved me over the phone, I still doubted his sincerity when he missed my birthday." He pressed his lips together, stayed quiet for a few moments. "I might have been three, four, five, but I remember it like it was yesterday."

"So how are you going to be different?" There was no need to point out he'd already abandoned her, just like his father had done.

"I'm trying to figure that out." He drew his free hand down her cheek.

Too much. Too. Much. Her insides crumbled at the light caress, a rockslide of emotion pummeling her gut. He could be so sweet. So loving. But his habit of leaving before anyone could leave him? She didn't know how she was going to live with that. It was no longer just her she needed to worry about. Her eyes stung. She opened them wide, then blinked to prevent any tears from forming. Time to change the subject. "You shouldn't touch me. Everyone's looking at us."

He traced one more tender circle before withdrawing his hand and rubbing his neck. "I came over here for a reason. We need to figure out our speeches for tomorrow, make sure our stories aren't overlapping or anything."

"Speechwriting? Wasn't that the excuse you gave for staying at my house after waterskiing? We both know how that ended."

A dry bark of laughter shook his shoulders. "This won't, I promise. Work only."

"Fine." Lauren sucked the dregs of her drink through her straw before handing the empty glass back to the bartender. "One more, please."

Tavish shot her a questioning look.

"God, Tavish, it's nonalcoholic. And if I can make it through a family wedding without anyone noticing I'm not drinking pinot grigio, I'll call it a win," she said.

Once she had a full glass in her hand and Tavish had a beer in his, he returned his hand right to that same drive-her-crazy place and guided her toward the house. "We'll have privacy in my mom's office."

Great. Just what she needed—privacy and Tavish Fitzgerald.

Chapter Eight

Tavish steered Lauren into his mother's office, an expansive, rectangular room with a solidly built mahogany desk in front of the draped window and a sitting area to one side. The walls held his mother's multitude of books: legal texts related to her work as an attorney, historical biographies, mystery novels. He might have gained his father's need to flee, but he'd also inherited his mother's adoration for the written word. He definitely preferred the latter trait.

What would he pass on to his child? Hopefully more than an eye for composition and a tendency for transience.

His heart panged as Lauren slid away from his hand and took a seat on one of the wide armchairs flanking a granite coffee table. Mile-high barriers erected with one cross of her gorgeous legs and a mask of a smile. She took her teeny purse from her shoulder and slipped a piece of paper from it. "So. Speeches."

He nodded, pulled a sheet of loose leaf from his back pocket and slung himself into the chair opposite her. "Hey. We're away from the crowd here. Away from our families. Relax."

"Okay." The word came out uncertain, but her shoulders sank against the back of the chair.

They haggled over who got to tell which embarrassing story, and remembered way too many good memories from growing up, from back when they'd first fallen in love with each other. For a half hour, things ceased to be about the present.

Mesmerized, Tavish took in Lauren as she scribbled edits onto her closing paragraph. She held her pen cap between her lips.

He really wanted to be that chunk of plastic.

A flash of the inevitable struck. "Screw it."

"Screw what?" The words came out garbled around the pen cap.

He leaned toward her, placed damp palms on the cool, rock tabletop. "If I were being crude, I'd suggest each other."

Green-gold eyes widened. Her lips fell open and the pen cap clattered to the table. "No. We can't. Terrible idea."

By the flush in her cheeks, and the temptation glistening in her eyes, she looked damn convincible.

He lowered his voice to a near whisper. "Terrible? Really?"

She nodded fervently, sending her ponytail swaying. "I wouldn't say terrible. Ill-advised, yeah. But we've never been less than spectacular in bed."

"That would complicate things even more."

His ex-wife wasn't just a pretty face. He'd always found her intelligence one of her more compelling traits.

And he was about to prove himself way less smart than she was. But she'd wanted honesty.

He could at least give her that.

"I love you, Lauren."

Mouth gaping, she stared at a point over his shoulder for a good minute. Finally, after he thought his heart would beat straight from his chest and out the door, disbelief lit her eyes. Her fingers loosened on the chair arms and the tips of her fingers turned pink again. "You mean you *did* love me."

"No, I mean I do love you. And now, with you carrying our child…" If he wasn't careful, what he felt for her would metamorphose right back into him being insanely *in* love with her. He moved to her side of the table, sat on the edge of the granite with his elbows on his knees. He captured her gaze with his. "We both know all the impossibilities, but for some God-only-knows reason, my feelings for you haven't, aren't and probably won't go away."

"That was grammatically incorrect," she breathed, sinking as far back as she could. "You could get your master's revoked for that."

"It got my point across. And stop trying to change the subject." Pinching one of the ruffles of her skirt, he teased the material between his fingertips.

Her teeth tugged her lip. The gauzy fabric on her tempting-as-sin breasts stretched as her breathing rate increased.

"All I'm saying is loving you is part of the equation for me," he said.

She leaned toward him, took his face between her palms. "We're crazy."

He groaned. That talented mouth, millimeters away from his skin. So close to touching. His tongue moistened his dry lips.

Crack. The door flew open and hit the wall.

Tavish jolted as his sister materialized in the doorway. Lauren's head jerked to look behind her. Her nails dug into his cheeks.

"Brother of mine! I've been looking for you everywhere." Mackenzie put a hand on her hip as she entered the room. Her eyes fixed on Lauren's hands, still cupping his face. "Oh. Jeez. Didn't mean to interrupt."

Lauren released him from her grip and stood up, turning so fast she wobbled on her heels. "You're not."

His sister crossed her arms. "Have you kissed and made up?" Pink bloomed on her cheeks. "Well, maybe not kissed. But made up."

"Yeah, we're good," he said, lying through his teeth but not seeing any other option.

The sigh Mackenzie released was loud enough he was surprised it didn't ruffle his hair from halfway across the room.

"Good enough," he clarified.

She crossed her arms and slid her gaze between Lauren and him. "Are you sure this is all in the past for you?"

"Our lifestyles are as incompatible now as they were last summer," he ground out. His seat on the coffee table put Lauren's right hand directly in his line of sight. She clenched it into a fist and the blood drained from her knuckles.

"That's not an exact answer to my question," Mackenzie said doggedly.

"It's the only answer you're getting."

It was all he could do not to reach for Lauren's tense fingers. To try to work them back to relaxation.

"I don't know why you think you can't grow roots, but I believe you can," his sister said.

His gut bottomed out. Her faith in him made no sense,

given how little he'd been around for the last decade. "Why? I've never proved that. Just like Dad couldn't."

"You're here now, aren't you? And you're staying to help after the wedding."

He shook his head. It was a nice thought, but he didn't share the same confidence in himself. Knew too intimately the skin-crawling feeling that prompted him to leave. That he ignored even now. "Do we seriously have to have this conversation?"

Her eyes narrowed in a you-owe-me glare. "Maybe you've changed."

Not unless he could alter his genetic code. "I don't think so."

Lauren let out a squeak. "I'm going to go find my brother."

"Lauren, wait." He reached out a hand to stop her but she evaded his attempt and swept from the room.

Mackenzie watched her friend leave and then glared daggers at him. "I think it was something you said."

"Gee, you think?"

"Yeah. And I think you're selling yourself short."

"No," he snapped. "We're just going to try to get through the weekend without stealing any more of the attention you and Drew rightly deserve."

"And then?" She sounded appreciative but suspicious.

"Then we're going to keep WiLA running. And when you're back, I'm gone." But not for as long as last time. He wanted to support Lauren where he could during her pregnancy. That would mean more frequent trips home. Even if he was suppressing his restlessness every second he was in town.

Mackenzie closed the space between them and sank into the seat Lauren had vacated. "I wish you'd stay." Her words spurted out like an arterial bleed.

"I'll come back."

"When? Two, four, six months from now?" Her voice took on a helpless tone. "You've only been home thirteen days of the last year."

Her arithmetic wormed its way under his skin, made him stiffen. "I didn't know you kept track."

She shot him a look of womanly scorn. "Of course I do."

He placed his palms on her knees and gave a squeeze. "I'll come back the minute you call me to say you're in labor. I'm going to take my uncle duties seriously. Someone's going to have to take some decent newborn portraits." And maybe by then he and Lauren would have a plan for their own child.

"I see." Mackenzie groaned as she eased back into the chair and toed out of her flats.

Concern panged at the sound of his sister's discomfort. "Are you okay?"

"Physically? Yeah."

"You're sure?" He examined her belly.

It twitched.

So did he. "How is that 'okay'?" Jesus, he had a lot to learn. With Lauren's medical background, she would know it all. And he'd probably end up feeling as incompetent supporting her through pregnancy as he did at the idea of becoming a father.

Mackenzie laughed. "That's normal. I'm pregnant with an active kid, is all." Her voice saddened. "I don't want a professional set of family photos taken on a brief visit home. I want you living in the same zip code as me."

"Kenz—"

"It's just… My old apartment's so close to my new house. You could live there for good. I could see you every day."

His throat tightened. Maybe he'd start using her place more often—he'd need some sort of home base if he was coming for visits with the baby—but it becoming his full-time residence? *Yikes.* Saying *I love you* was one thing. Living it was something he'd never quite managed to do. And he had just over seven months to learn.

The next morning Lauren dressed in her turquoise maid-of-honor gown. It felt tighter than yesterday. Had to be her imagination, or maybe discomfort from morning sickness. She was weeks away from showing. Ugh, if only she wasn't so pale against the vibrant shantung silk. She'd applied as much blush as she could without looking like a clown, but somehow last night had sucked all the color from her cheeks.

It was still only seven forty and Mackenzie had wanted to sleep until eight, but Lauren hadn't been able to follow her friend's lead. She'd been awake, staring at the ceiling for hours. Because the wedding dress code was reasonably casual, they'd decided to do their own hair and makeup. Lauren had pulled her hair back into a French twist. Pinned in tight. Just like her willpower to get through the next sixteen hours without falling apart.

Step one: avoid all thoughts of the words *I* and *love* and *you* being uttered by her fricking ex-husband.

Step two: well, no need to get carried away. Step one was going to take enough of her energy.

She brushed her hands over the below-the-knee hemline and took stock of her situation. Still pregnant. Her sister still hadn't spoken to her.

And Tavish still loved her.

Which was part of his *equation*.

But so was the fact he didn't think he'd changed. Seriously, how could someone hear they were going to become a parent and not change in some way?

She swallowed, trying to make the tension in her throat spread to her heart, provide some firm support for the day. If she managed to crawl into bed tonight retaining any semblance of emotional wholeness, she'd head straight for the convenience store and buy a Powerball ticket.

She glanced in Gwen Fitzgerald's main bathroom mirror one last time to make sure her all-day lip gloss hadn't adhered itself to her teeth, then made her way to the kitchen. Cadie, Mackenzie and she had stayed overnight after the rehearsal dinner. Mackenzie had slept in her old bedroom and Cadie and Ben had stayed in the main guest room, leaving Lauren lucky—*ha! There's that joke of a word again*—enough to spend the night in Tavish's old room. The collection of memories he'd taped over his bed—tickets from the Garth Brooks concert he'd taken her to in Missoula, his acceptance letter to Yale, a roll of camera film he'd refused to develop or tell her what was on it—had long disappeared. But the memory of him had spooned up against her, keeping her awake until the wee morning hours.

Hoping the bags under her eyes were disguised by the careful application of concealer, she sat down at the kitchen table with her sister, who was busy feeding a sleeper-clad Ben yogurt and applesauce. Cadie wore her bridesmaid's dress, identical to Lauren's, but had buttoned a men's Oxford shirt over the satin.

One of Sam's? Couldn't be. Her sister hadn't brought more than a box of her late husband's belongings when she'd moved home from Colorado. She swam in the garment, still way too thin even a year and a bit after being widowed. Jeez, on the summit of the mountain, where the ceremony was to take place, she'd blow over if a gust hit her.

"Sexy shirt," Lauren teased.

Cadie glanced down at her front, then back up at Lauren. Her lips pressed into a line and indecision flashed across her face before she cleared her throat. "Perfect for the ceremony, right? I know the light blue isn't quite the same as the turquoise, but it's close enough. I found it in Gwen's guest closet."

"It'll work awesome for pictures." She drummed her fingers against the table. "Can we talk, Cades?"

Her sister's smile stretched her skin across her jaw, cast hollows in her cheeks. "You didn't need me—didn't want to—and that hurts. But we shouldn't think about it today."

Lauren drew back. "But I do need your help."

"Don't force the issue just to make up."

"I'm not." It wasn't about finding something random to confess in order to make up with her sister. She needed Cadie as a confidante, damn it. There was no one else to talk to about Tavish.

"Yeah?" Cadie spooned another tiny heap of applesauce into Ben's surprisingly clean mouth, sounding cautiously hopeful. "Ready to stop treating me like I'm going to fall apart?"

"Yeah. I just didn't think you needed to worry about me. Didn't want to be your tipping point."

"Ah." Cadie switched containers and scooped yogurt onto the spoon. She let out a frustrated breath. "I'm not helpless, Lauren. And I don't get why you became the mama bear."

"Someone needed to be."

Her sister studied the floor. "You're not Mom, Lauren."

"I know that."

"Do you?" Cadie looked up, stared straight into all of Lauren's dark, ugly corners.

"Uh-huh." She couldn't get the sound out with the convincingness she wanted. "No one could be like Mom."

"No one *needs* to be like Mom."

Her chest tightened. She couldn't quite bring herself to agree.

Letting out a long breath, Cadie fed Ben the last scrapings from the bowl of applesauce. "It's too much effort to stay mad at family. I'll probably be hurt for a while, but it's impossible not to forgive you, Laur. But tell me something. When did you start sleeping with Tavish again?"

Lauren's jaw hit her lap. She reflexively touched her stomach—obviously still flat, so Cadie hadn't figured out about her failed attempt at closure that way. "I— What do you mean?"

"Come on," her sister scoffed. "The way he was looking at you last night? The way you were looking at him? No way has it been a year since you've done the dirty deed."

"Uh…" She wasn't going to lie to her sister again, but she couldn't make her voice work to admit the truth.

Cadie wiped Ben's face with a wet cloth and took her babbling son out of the old high chair Gwen had unearthed from the attic. Bouncing Ben on her lap, she pierced Lauren with a saberlike gaze. "You're not the only person who's worried about her sister. It's not exactly easy to mend a broken heart."

"My heart's already broken, Cadie. It can't get worse."

Cadie's look of disbelief was clear, and echoed the warnings in Lauren's gut. "Falling in love with someone twice isn't worse than doing it once?"

Not when you'd never stopped loving the person. But

loving Tavish wasn't enough. Hadn't been then, wouldn't be now. The day of her grandparents' funeral, he'd sat in his thinking place, a pleading look stretching his handsome face. *I can't take pictures of Montana forever.* And then the clincher: *Please. Love me enough to come with me.*

She'd said no.

And now her pregnancy made following him doubly impossible.

But living with the look of devastation she'd put on his face was no easier a year after the fact. Words tumbled out before she could stop it. "Memorial Day weekend. When he was home, we…"

"Made love—"

"Had sex."

"Semantics." Cadie waved a hand. "I think you love him, so it's making love."

It so had been. "I'm not going to disagree."

Ben tugged at one of Cadie's loose curls. Cadie untangled his fingers from her hair and kissed his fingertips. And Lauren flashed forward a year or two, to having her own baby. Alone, like her sister.

Her stomach rolled and she wrapped her arms around her midsection. "You want me to confide in you? Here goes—I'm pregnant."

Cadie froze, the only movement in her body the long, slow blink of her eyelids. Even Ben's tiny palm smacking her on the nose didn't get her moving.

"It's not that big a deal," Lauren joked, though the poor attempt at humor came out way too wobbly to be worthy of a laugh.

"You're pregnant."

"Yeah. I have a bone to pick with a certain prophylactic company."

Cadie shook her head. "Does he know?"

"Yeah."

"What are you going to do?"

"We haven't gotten that far." Lauren's heart clamored, made her want to rip the traitorous thing right out of her chest. Beyond its physiological necessity, the organ had been way too much trouble as of late. "He says he wants to be involved. But he also insists he can't settle in town." She scrubbed her fingers over her mouth, then stopped. Stupid nervous reaction, making her smear her lip gloss.

"That's a bit contradictory," Cadie said carefully, plunking Ben's diaper-cushioned bottom on the table in front of her.

"Just a little." Lauren fisted an abandoned paper napkin and began to worry the edges. "Get this—he says he loves me."

"He probably does," Cadie ventured. "But the way he loves and the way you need to be loved don't line up."

A wave of anxiety knocked Lauren off kilter. Were they too misaligned to even function as parents? "So what do I do?"

"It's not about what you do, Laur. It's about what he does. If he's going to say he loves you and wants to be involved, then he needs to prove that to you."

And that would be great and all, provided he was able to prove himself. But if he tried and failed, she didn't know if she could put herself back together again. Or if she talked to him about it and he refused to even try—for her, or their child—what would she do then?

Before Lauren could reply, Mackenzie entered the kitchen wearing a thin, knee-length bathrobe tied over her bump. "This looks like way too serious a conversation for my wedding morning." She grinned and placed her hands on the sides of her stomach. "You both look great. And I'm about to, as soon as I feed the poppy seed."

Cadie looked at Mackenzie's stomach and then pointedly at Lauren, but didn't say anything to break her confidence. "Kenz, don't get me wrong. You're stunning and gorgeous and every synonym for beautiful in the entire world. But that baby you're carrying is way too big to be referred to as a poppy seed anymore."

For the rest of the morning they fought with Mackenzie and Cadie's curls, got their fingers stuck together with false eyelash glue and interspersed the curses that followed with a whole lot of laughs. Plenty to occupy Lauren's attention. But keeping her mind on wedding prep involved more effort than she was capable of. The possibility of Tavish proving he loved her and wanting to be involved in raising their baby consumed her, refused to go away.

A wildflower carpet ringed the grassy area where, framed by summer-bare peaks, Drew and Mackenzie kissed at the end of their wedding ceremony. Tavish watched with stinging eyes, but hadn't heard a word. The script from his own vows, long since memorized, played on a loop in his head.

Love. Honor. Cherish.

Funny how fulfilling those vows had meant breaking off his marriage.

But the baby meant reconnecting in some way. It wasn't going to be as lovers or partners in the true sense of the word—nothing like having your *I love you* replied to with *We're crazy*—but there was still an intimacy involved in being parents.

The recessional music started and he pressed pause on the mental tape before it drove him totally insane.

Making eye contact with his ex-wife, he met her in the center of the altar and took her hand in the crook of his arm. They followed the bride and groom down the aisle.

It was utterly impossible to retreat from an altar with Lauren without envisioning her face when the organist at the little chapel on the Strip had struck up the beginning notes of "Can't Help Falling in Love with You." Lauren's hair still smelled sultry, tropical, like swimming under a Hawaiian waterfall. The scent wafted at him on the mountain breeze. Then, he'd wrecked her fussy up-do not five minutes after they'd left the chapel. That limousine ride...

He interrupted his memories with a string of silent swearing. Nine hours to go. Sure, they'd be working together for the next couple of weeks, but at least they wouldn't be thinking about weddings the whole time.

No, we'll be thinking about babies.

An incongruent blend of excitement and terror climbed into his throat as they approached the end of the aisle.

"Everyone's looking at us," Lauren whispered.

He slowed his pace to accommodate her. Her stupidly impractical—but atrociously sexy—shoes looked to be getting stuck in the ground.

"Well, you're starting to get that rosy pregnant glow," he replied, voice just as quiet as hers.

She flushed, hissed out a shush.

He cleared his throat, which had clogged as soon as he'd connected Lauren and pregnant and glow. "You're too easy to tease, sweetheart."

"I'm not in the mood." She dug her fingers into his arm. "I'm already having a hard time thinking about anything but embryos this morning without you bringing it up."

Blinding him with science. She was so damn sexy.

"Hey. Put it aside for the moment. Enjoy Mackenzie and Drew's day."

"You sound calm." She didn't. Confused, sure. Panicky, definitely.

"Mission accomplished," he muttered.

They headed for the location Mackenzie and Drew had chosen for their pictures, a wooden-railed viewpoint with a stunning vista of Sutter Creek and Moosehorn Lake. Teetering on her high heels as she followed the tree-lined path, Lauren linked her hands around his forearm. "These pictures will be beautiful, but I might break my ankle in the process."

He untangled his arm from her grasp and gripped her around her shoulders. "I could carry you."

She stopped walking, jaw hanging open as if he'd lost his mind.

Not far from the truth, really. "What? Drew picked up Mackenzie fifty yards back." The happy couple were the only ones ahead of them. The wedding guests were heading for the chairlift that would take them down to the cocktail party at the mid-station Creekview Lodge, and his mother and Edward Dawson trailed behind with Cadie, Ben and the slow-moving, injured Zach Cardenas.

"They just got married, Tavish. He's supposed to carry her around. If you did the same for me, people would talk. They already are, I'm sure."

"No one cares what we do, Lauren." He figured if he said the words with enough force, they'd become true. "Did you enjoy the ceremony?"

She gripped his arm tighter and started walking again, gaze affixed to the ground. "You wrecked it for me."

"Huh?" He figured between holding her up on their walk down the aisle, and helping her along now, all he'd done was stop her from falling over.

"I kept getting distracted by the mental picture of looking like Mackenzie come winter."

Tavish's gut tensed. "My thoughts might have drifted in that direction over the past forty-eight hours."

They walked silently for twenty more yards or so until they caught up to Mackenzie and Drew and the wedding photographer. Having their pictures taken prevented them from having any more private conversations. As much as he would have loved to, with being in the wedding party Tavish wasn't able to do all the photography for the wedding, but he did take the portraits of Mackenzie and Drew by themselves. As he snapped frame after frame, he recognized the looks of bliss on their faces as the same one he'd worn for the first five days of his own marriage. But they would manage to make those looks stick. Wouldn't fail like Tavish had.

Chapter Nine

In the corner of the turquoise-spritzed lounge of the Creekview Lodge, a pair of musicians played an acoustic guitar rendition of "Bewitched, Bothered and Bewildered." Lauren decided it was her theme song. She fit the definitions of all three of those words, and was closing in on bedraggled, beleaguered and besieged. Her hair had wilted during the speeches, and she was tired of talking to people who were being overly polite and obviously not asking her about Tavish. All the while their eyes glinted with curiosity.

Lauren sneaked out one of the sliding doors onto the balcony. She didn't begrudge her brother his lot in life, swaying to the music with his new wife. He deserved to fall in love and be happy about fatherhood and marriage and having a job he loved. But everything about today reminded her about how she had the opposite.

There was no point in falling in love with Tavish

again. Parenthood would be mostly on her shoulders—he'd float in between trips to maintain a connection with their child, but not with her. Cadie was right: Tavish saying he loved her wasn't enough. The words needed actions to mean anything.

The night air, still warm despite the setting sun, provided no relief from the sweat trickling under her strapless bra. She skirted behind the cluster of chairs arranged for the post-dusk fireworks and headed to one of the wooden staircases. Diamond-patterned metal grates lined the steps. Necessary to stop skiers from slipping, but treacherous for summer heels. Clinging to the cedar railing, she minced her way from the deck to the ground below. She didn't want to miss the fireworks, but wanted to watch them alone. She squinted in the dim light and found her way around to the picnic tables on the west side of the building. Climbing onto the nearest table of the group, she hiked her dress up enough to allow her to sit cross-legged. She tugged off her shoes and rubbed the balls of her feet.

As perfect as things were going to get. Removing articles of clothing couldn't alleviate the ache in her chest.

The sunset blended peach into pink into mauve, a gift for the eyes. Tavish could do wonders with this display of color. How could someone so capable of capturing beauty not be willing to create the wonder of a marriage or a united family? But deep down she knew why. It wasn't that he didn't want to. It was that he didn't believe he could. If time travel were possible, going back a few decades and tearing a strip off Tavish's father for having jerked his family around would be one of her first stops. But fantasizing wouldn't actually result in Tavish dealing with his issues. In him being an equal, committed partner.

Her eyes welled. Pulling her legs to her chest, she dropped her forehead onto her knees. The silk hem of her dress substituted for a tissue, absorbing her tears. She gently dabbed at her eyes with her fingertips. Her waterproof mascara would hold out, but the soft, brown eyeshadow was a goner. She gave up trying to look good and wiped with her thumbs until no trace of tears remained on her face.

The crunch of dress shoes on dirt approached from around the corner of the lodge.

She didn't need to ask who it was. Struggling to control her jagged breathing, she raised her voice to make sure it carried. "You followed me?"

"Yeah," Tavish called, voice low. He finally appeared—all half-disassembled tuxedo, rangy body and chiding expression. "You shouldn't be out here by yourself. You might run into a bear. And no one has any reason to come to this side of the building."

"That was the point. And I'd rather take on a bear than wedding guests."

"Me, too." Hands jammed into his pants' pockets, he stopped in front of the table. He'd lost his jacket after the speeches, and had removed his tie and rolled up his shirtsleeves since she'd last seen him dancing with his mother. *Too freaking sexy.* She cleared her throat. "You weren't bamboozled into getting the show preserved in pictures?"

"Bamboozled?" A grin spilled light into his eyes. He climbed up on the table and settled behind her. His bent legs cradled her own. "No, my camera's retired for the night. The other photographer is competent enough."

She stayed tilted forward—though tempting, leaning back was a display of affection that would lead into dangerous territory. He rested his hands on her shoulders, massaging them with capable fingers.

Her flesh heated, went pliable. She stifled the moan threatening to erupt.

He pressed a thumb into a tender knot.

"Ahh," she groaned.

"Sorry. You're tight."

Yup, her muscles were wound to match her brain. "And I came out here to get some time away from everyone. Including you." *Especially you.* "No offense. But I'm hitting my limit for the day."

His hands stilled, solid and warm on her bare shoulders. "Guess I didn't help matters last night."

Her disbelieving snort echoed across the picnic area.

Dropping his forehead between her shoulder blades, he exhaled. "Hopefully, I won't make as much of a mess of helping out with your family's business as I have of our personal lives. Not that I'm taking *all* the credit here. It's unfortunate we can't find middle ground. But that's not new."

His words lacked true inflection, sounded over-rehearsed. As speeches went, she'd preferred his first of the evening, when he'd sweetly toasted his sister. She reached back with a hand, wove her fingers into his wavy mess of hair. "It's not about middle ground anymore. It's about creating security for our child."

"I know," he murmured. His hand slid from her shoulders to settle low on her belly.

Oh, that felt too good. Not in a tearing-clothes-off kind of way. No, Tavish's palm caressing her stomach felt like Sunday mornings in cozy pajama pants with animal-shaped pancakes and a sippy cup of apple juice alongside their mugs of coffee.

So a lie, then. It feels like a lie.

The brief spate of pleasure drained from her body. Losing the energy to keep herself upright, she leaned against his hard chest. His arms encircled her. Fingers finding purchase on his wrists, she teased the light dusting of hair and warm skin. The links of his bracelet were warm from the heat of his body.

She studied the piece closely. White and yellow-gold strips, bent and fused together in an irregular design, made a series of modern, Celtic-like knots. Only two twisted links, one thinner than the other, were identical in pattern. A pattern etched into her memory as she'd worn it on her own finger for a short-but-unforgettable spell.

"Tavish." Her voice echoed hollow from her chest. "These are our wedding rings."

"Yep," he murmured. His lips came to rest on the back of her hairline at the base of her French twist.

"You're still wearing your wedding band?" *And mine?*

"Not exactly. I took it off my finger." He traced the backs of his fingers down her shock-frozen cheek. "But somehow I couldn't let go of it."

Don't ask. You don't want to know. You don't *want to know.* "Why?"

Damn it.

"I couldn't let go of the last thing I had of you." He nuzzled her ear, buried his brow in the curve of her neck.

The need to reiterate her position, more to remind herself of her commitments rather than to remind Tavish, built up until it spilled out of her mouth in a torrent. "Love's not just feeling, it's doing, too. I'm not saying you need to be here every second of every day to be a good father, but you need to figure out some sort of regular visitation. Something concrete, dependable.

"I'm not going anywhere—I've got my job and my family. I have to mend the rift I've caused, prove I'm there for them. Re-establish my equilibrium well before the baby arrives. Their support will be critical as my pregnancy progresses and after the birth. But if you can figure out a way for us to have your support, too..."

"So stop thinking and start acting?" Tavish said, tone thoughtful. He splayed one big hand across her abdomen and slid the other up to cup one of her breasts. Languid heat ambled down her limbs, saturated her fingers and toes until they felt like lead weights. "Works for me."

She groaned. "We can't..."

"I'm not suggesting we make love, Lauren." One of his fingers circled her nipple and even through her dress and her bra it sent shockwaves of pleasure through her body. "But keeping my hands entirely to myself seems a shame."

"We're in a pretty public place..."

The first few bursts of fireworks thundered above them. "No one's coming around here. Terrible view of the show." Sliding out from behind her, he laid her down gently and climbed off the table. Excitement bordering on frenzied need tore through her as he stood at the end of the table and stroked callused fingertips along the insides of her thighs. "Awesome view for me, though."

Rising up on her elbows, she stared at him as the heat of a flush spread from her thighs to her belly to her breasts. "What are you doing?"

Tavish braced a hand next to her body and brushed his other thumb along her cheekbone, pulling her in to share a kiss that melted her insides. "You wanted actions over words."

"This isn't the kind of action I meant."

"I'll try what you meant. But I want this, too." His words weighed her down, and she sank against the hard wooden tabletop, destroyed by the powerless hunger in his gaze. "You... I can't..."

"You can, sweetheart. Open for me."

Whimpering, she let her legs fall to the sides. A thrill swirled in her core at seeing him on his knees. Eyes shuttered, he held her gaze as he sneaked her panties to the side. His thumb dipped into her center, and she bit her lip as her needy flesh throbbed around the sweet abrasion, then spasmed in complaint when he withdrew.

He settled his palms on the very tops of her thighs. "What do you want, Pixie?"

Her pleasure dulled at his words. She wanted all of him. Every day, every minute. She couldn't have that. But she could have him for a moment. And what a moment it would be. "I want your mouth."

The tawny curls on his head, lit with flecks of red and blue and green from the fireworks overhead, lowered to her most sensitive place. Hot breath panted against her skin. "Here?"

"Close."

She could feel him smile against her sex as he pressed the barest of kisses to her aching want. "Here?"

"Closer."

"Here, then." Spreading her with his thumbs, he ran his tongue along her slick flesh.

Raw currents of pleasure poured through her as she went tense and boneless all at the same time. She wanted completion, but this was too good to rush. Nothing mattered more than the aching press of his mouth against her center, of his tender hands loving her as if she were the best gift he could ever be given. Her body didn't care about the impossibilities, only registered the perfection of having his tongue curving around her sensitive, wet bud. Her muscles strained and her back arched. "Tavish!"

"Let go, Pixie." And his skilled fingers and mouth wouldn't let her do anything but.

She forgot about everything, a blessed gift, as he tormented and touched her until she dissolved under a sheet of white light. Booming fireworks covered the sound of her release.

"I love making you gasp my name," he mumbled. His breath came out in rushed gusts as he rested his cheek on her stomach.

"Mmm."

He righted her panties and tugged her skirt back into place. Utterly sated, she sent him a wobbly smile.

"Love making you smile, too." His expression faltered. The satisfaction dimmed in his eyes. And in that moment, she could almost read his mind.

If only it was always this easy.

By the end of Monday, after spending the morning at the outdoor rock-climbing facility and the afternoon polishing up winter brochures for the ski school, Tavish's mind hummed. It might not be the same as facing off with a polar bear with only his camera as a buffer, but working for WiLA had kept him engaged all day long. So much so he'd gone out after his shift and taken a series of pictures better than any of the work he'd done in Russia over the winter.

Inspired, and shocked by how much he wasn't hating life in Sutter Creek, he picked up the office phone and dialed the department head of Media and Theatre Arts at Montana State. *Nothing serious. Just putting feelers out.* Lauren wanted proof that his relationship with their baby would have some stability to it. And the thought of his child growing up with any of the doubt he himself had borne crushed his chest like a boulder. He couldn't always be around. But he could work on making his schedule more predictable. And maybe pick up some work closer to home for part of the year.

Dropping his name ranked as one of the more obnoxious ways to start a conversation, but it did get him the department head's direct line PDQ.

As soon as the receptionist put him on hold, he started doubting his decision. *Hang up. Hang up.*

His hand refused the command.

"Bob Davenport speaking."

Tavish vaguely recalled the man's name from somewhere, but the people he'd met over the course of his career were too numerous to always put a face to. "Good afternoon, Dr. Davenport. This is Tavish Fitzgerald. Thanks for taking my call."

"I know your work well. And call me Bob. What can I do for you?"

Hang up. Hang up. "I'm wondering if you have any positions coming up on your faculty in the near future."

That was the opposite of hanging up. *Argh.*

"Well." Bob Davenport sounded flabbergasted. "We don't have any specific positions… Were you looking for full-time?"

"No. Not at all. Maybe two courses a year, max. Preferably to do with environmental photography. Getting the message of a cause, an emergency, across in a few frames."

"No political causes?"

"I could teach it. But I'm not going to accept any more of those assignments." Tavish used to get a rush from war zones and unstable regions. But getting killed by an IED while on assignment was no longer an option. He couldn't promise to always be in Sutter Creek, but he could at least do his best to stay alive.

Davenport hummed thoughtfully. "Do you have a master's degree?"

"Yes, from Yale."

"Good, good. Send me something on paper, but you're plenty qualified with that degree."

"I figured. And I'm interested in settling semipermanently into the area now." The words were coming out of their own volition. They had to be.

"I have to say, I'd scrounge up some money to make room for you. I can't offer you a permanent position, but you could come in as an artist-in-residence. It would involve teaching seminars, supervising some student projects, and would give you some time to continue with your own work. The salary is by no means substantial..."

Ah, academics. Tavish had a feeling the hiring process wasn't as simple as Bob Davenport made it sound. Then again, it didn't matter if it didn't turn out. This was an exploratory call, not a commitment. "I'm not worried about the money. I'll keep doing location work."

"When would you want to start?"

"My schedule's clear come November. I could be yours for the winter session."

Holy hell. He blinked, floored by his own statement. The winter session? Talk about a way bigger step than he'd been intending on taking today. *How's that for action, Lauren?*

"I don't want to get ahead of myself, but I feel good about it," the other man said.

The receiver vibrated against Tavish's ear as his hand started to shake.

"I'm going to make this happen," Davenport continued. "We can't pass up someone of your caliber."

Sweat beaded on Tavish's forehead and dampened his T-shirt despite the air-conditioning. "Thank you for the compliment," he choked out.

"I'll call you back as soon as I figure out logistics. Give me a few days."

They exchanged cordial goodbyes, then hung up.

Tavish stared at the phone. That had been too damn easy.

He'd completed his masters to get more credibility behind his name, but maybe it would come in handy, provide him with a challenging and productive job in Montana. One that would still allow him to work abroad. Hope blossomed in his chest. He could experiment with how many assignments he had to take in a year in order not to feel like he was crawling out of his skin in Sutter Creek. Half the year here, half away, maybe.

He closed his eyes. Defeat erased his desperate attempts to be positive. The urge to leave would come. Maybe not as often as in previous years. But enough to be a wall between him and Lauren. Half a year. How could that possibly be enough?

But how could he not at least try?

Chapter Ten

Lauren trudged toward the base lodge early Monday evening, giving mental kudos to her brother. Running WiLA was a pile of fun, but that fun came with a fair degree of challenge. So far today she'd juggled staff scheduling requests, put out fires with a bookings glitch and called in a maintenance crew when a fuel injector had crapped out on the Peak Chair's prime mover. However, it was better than suturing wounds.

No. Dealing with a fricking diesel engine is not *better than medicine.* She shoved the door of her brother's office in the basement of the main lodge and held back a groan as it swung open.

Tavish sat at Zach Cardenas's desk, studying a sketchbook. She'd been hoping for some time to herself to end the day, but no, no reprieve for her.

Probably a good thing given they needed to talk about what had happened at the reception, though knowing a conversation was necessary didn't mean she actually *wanted* to have it. Maybe he expected quid pro quo for how well he'd pleasured her on that picnic table. It would only be fair. That table, or maybe his tongue, merited being bronzed. But though they'd walked back to the lodge hand in hand—separating before they'd run into any guests, mind you—she hadn't seen him yesterday. This morning, he'd kept things super light between them, greeting her with an exaggerated, sexy grin and a comment about getting to play secretary to the boss. Did he intend to end the day in the same vein?

Slumped in his chair, he lacked his customary, just-shy-of-arrogant confidence. He greeted her with a bare nod. No more teasing, then. Whatever was on his page was demanding his full attention.

She straightened her hiking shorts and perched herself on the corner of his desk. "Where's my end-of-the-day innuendo? It perked me up better than a coffee this morning," she teased.

He lifted a shoulder and traced her knee with the pencil in his hand. "Just tired."

Based on the color in his cheeks and the lack of smudges under his eyes, she doubted it. "You sure?"

"Yeah." He ran his hand through his hair. "I just got off the phone with…work stuff. Got me a little edgy, I guess." Dropping his pencil on the desk, he traced her knee with the tip of his finger instead.

Her breathing kicked up a notch. She linked her fingers with his to prevent him from traveling closer to the hem of her shorts. Hyperventilating would not project an I-can-take-you-or-leave-you image.

Leaning forward, she caught a better view of his creation, which looked like his thinking place. She'd last been there with him after her grandparents' funeral.

She'd been distraught and he'd used his skillful hands and mouth to get her mind off her grief. Then they'd argued.

And he'd left.

Just like he'll leave in a few weeks. She forced the thought to linger, let the full weight of it settle on her shoulders. "Can I see?"

His guarded eyes studied her for a moment before he passed the book to her with a flick of his wrist. "I guess."

Lauren rotated the pad. The flowing water was indelibly and precisely etched. Alive on the page. "Tavish," she breathed. "This is incredible."

He shrugged. "Fine arts electives came in handy. I can create something decent with most art materials."

"This is beyond decent. You could sell this. I feel like I could put my hand through the page and bring it out dripping."

"Thanks for the compliment, but I couldn't sell my sketches."

"But drawings and photography are both art. And you're gifted in both media."

"I'm not above selling my art. Obviously. But that—" he pointed at his sketchbook with the unsharpened end of his pencil "—that's me. I don't sell myself."

"I can see your heart in this, definitely. I think I get what you mean." She flipped the page.

And was staring into a mirror.

Her breath caught in her throat. "Oh, my God."

She tried to breathe evenly. He'd rendered her face with such detail, such reverence. If his art was a part of him, then did he consider her a part of him still?

"Tavish." She traced a finger along the two-dimensional replica of her nose.

He kept his gaze on his tented fingers in his lap. "Your eyes are the same color as the river as it changes from

shallow to deep. I was at that spot, and remembered…"
Turning red, he looked around the room with a panicked
jerk to his motions. He stood and grabbed a clipboard. "I
have to go debrief with the rafting folks."

He bolted through the door faster than the river at
spring melt, leaving Lauren holding a mirror-image picture of herself but no longer knowing who she was beneath the surface.

Straggling into the WiLA office two days later, Lauren collapsed into the office chair. Hump day number one
was over, and she was pleased with how she'd done so
far. Andrew's job was mainly supervisory, but like her
brother, she couldn't help but get involved in operations.
She'd have preferred to actually do some of the guiding,
but being pregnant precluded buckling on a climbing har-
ness. Tavish had filled in the gaps where necessary—they
made a good team. On the job, at least.

A single daisy, stuck in a water glass next to her key-
board, drew her attention to a sticky note attached to the
flat-screen computer monitor.

Meet me at my place at 7.

My place.
Huh. Up until now, Tavish had always called the pretty
apartment just off Main Street "Mackenzie's place." Lauren sank farther into the chair. Why did he have to tease
her with little steps toward growing roots? It didn't matter how many little steps he took—he wouldn't be able
to make the big leaps.

Don't forget that. If they were going to function together as parents, they had to resist their emotions—and
their physical pull. So what if he still kinda-sorta wore

their wedding rings? She still hadn't convinced him to stay put in Sutter Creek.

But...my place...?

No. She couldn't count on him.

Stay firm.

She recited the words to herself as she closed up and headed home. As she changed into a T-shirt and a stretchy skirt that skimmed her knees. As she drove to Tavish's, and especially when she read the Post-it note on his door, written in the same bold print as before.

Come on in, sweetheart.

Her internal stay-firm mantra wavered in the face of his words, the confidence of his penmanship. And when she cautiously opened the door, walked through the entryway into the high-ceilinged living and dining area, the chant shriveled and died.

All of Mackenzie's old furniture—gone. She stroked her hand along the back of the polished leather couch. He'd decorated with raw-wood coffee and end tables and a Peruvian rug. A square dining table filled the other end of the rectangular room. Some late-nineties rock played quietly from the docking station on a tall, wide bookshelf next to the unlit fireplace. An assortment of hardcovers and paperbacks stood on the half-filled shelves.

And the art—a fist of emotion gripped her throat when she realized he'd personalized the walls. An eclectic blend of his photography—the sharp angles of New York City architecture, the twirling spires of Eastern Europe, the towering ice of Antarctica—mixed in with internationally flavored prints. Every single item a piece of Tavish.

Her eye was drawn to the mantel. Oh, sweet Lord. Two

framed pictures were nestled with a collection of colored rocks. One of Andrew and him hanging off a rock face, and one of Mackenzie, their mom and him at Mackenzie's wedding that he'd clearly had printed in the last few days. She said silent thanks for the fact he hadn't put up a picture of her—that would have reduced her to a helpless puddle of skin and bones and need.

"Lauren?"

She spun. "Hey."

He stood in the doorway to the little galley kitchen with a tomato-splattered dish towel tucked into the waist of his jeans. One muscle-roped arm braced against the door frame. Good God. The human body was a marvel, and Tavish's, with all its long lines and hard definition, never disappointed. Desire curled in her belly, stirring against her fascination with every part of him. Her confusion rolled into a great, brewing, uncontainable churn.

His eyes gleamed. "Hungry?"

"Sure." For more than food. She cleared her throat. "I like what you've done with the place."

"Thanks. I'll need to have a home base for the sake of the baby, and this works. I thought I could put a crib and stuff in the spare room."

Unsettling reality encroached on the happiness from seeing his personal mark on the apartment. Why hadn't she considered the separation involved in coparenting—him having his time with the baby, her having her time? Dealing with custody and deciding who got what weekend and arguing over holidays? Her stomach rolled worse than from morning sickness.

His brow wrinkled. "Isn't this what you wanted, Lauren? Me, showing some consistency?"

"Well, yeah, but—" She bit her lip.

"But...?"

But what she said she wanted and what she really wanted were two different things. Him making changes to support her and to love their baby checked boxes but didn't actually fill her soul.

"I love you," she blurted. Holding herself up under his startled, steaming gaze, she balled her fingers into fists and fought the hot moisture pricking the corners of her eyes.

"I love you, too." Tavish took two long strides and gathered her into his strong arms. Kept her upright as her legs turned to gelatin. She gripped handfuls of the back of his soft T-shirt and lost her grip on her tears.

"Hey, shh." He stroked a gentle hand through her loose-hanging hair. "We'll figure something out."

His shirt muffled her "How?"

"We'd intended to compromise before—we can do it again. Maybe you and the baby can travel with me sometimes. Your family isn't asking as much of you as they did last year—"

"No." She leaned back and wiped her eyes before staring into his. The hope glinting there shattered her heart. "It's not about what they expect from me. It's about what I expect of myself. And I want to be here for them. Nor will I be able to leave the clinic for long stretches of time."

Music from the docking station filled the hollow silence of the room. Failed to fill the hollowness of her heart.

Tavish didn't say anything, just pressed his fingertips into the base of her spine.

"We might be able to manage if you only left for two or three months a year."

Dropping his hands from her body, he jammed his fingers into his hair, squeezed at the messy strands. "I was thinking more half and half. But I'm trying, Lauren. I even called about taking a part-time position at Montana State—"

"You did?" Losing control over her jaw, she stared at him, hands hanging limply at her sides. Staying resolute was so much easier when it was all his fault. But now— the apartment, the job…

Tavish's forehead wrinkled. "Yeah, I did. I can't put our child through what I was put through. I know you're not willing to come with me when I work—can we come up with a different solution?"

She could barely look at him, so sweet and hot and staring at her with challenge flashing in his eyes. "You left me last time. You will again."

Was that her voice, that desperate, shrill noise?

Anytime she'd heard that tone come from anyone else, she'd viewed it as a sign of stubborn irrationality. That couldn't be the truth in her case—her devotion to her family and the clinic wasn't irrational. Tavish changing his life only affected Tavish. A compromise by her had the potential to hurt the baby, her dad, Cadie… They needed her to be here, to support them. And she had to follow through on her promise to her mom, follow through with the clinic. She pressed both hands over her heart in an attempt to quell the ache in her chest.

Tavish let out a gust of air. With a slight nod of his head, he said, "You're right. I'll eventually leave. But this time, I'll come back."

"And a part-time relationship between us is no less plausible now than it was last year."

"Not unless you're willing to sever the umbilical cord between you and your dad—"

"Enough." She cut him off before he could hammer any further dents into her reasoning. The professional in her started to nag that she was nearing the definition of phobic, but she ignored it. Wanting her family happy and safe was not a phobia. It wasn't. She'd seen what happened when she acted selfishly. "Do you remember where I was when my mom's surgery went sideways? At summer camp, having a grand old time. And when my grandfather was dead on the side of the road, my grandmother in a coma, I was off marrying you. Pretending that it was okay for me to have given up the plans I'd made with my mom before she died." She rambled on, desperate for him to understand. "I won't put myself before my family again. My dad and Cadie need me here. And the baby will need that stability, too."

"And what if I need you?"

His pleading whisper pushed her over the edge. "I have to go." She crossed her arms, tried to hold in the blood from the verbal knife he'd just shoved between her ribs. He needed to stop looking at her like he was tearing into pieces. She couldn't handle it. Because he was compromising. He was trying.

Which only made it obvious how much she wasn't able to do the same.

Backing toward the front door, she said the only thing she knew would make him shut up, make him close off. "Call me if you decide you love me enough to put me ahead of your job."

Chapter Eleven

"Lauren Dawson? Come in, Lauren Dawson." Tavish had arrived at work today intending to press her more after she'd bolted from his apartment last night. They'd made eye contact at a morning staff debriefing but she'd run off the second the meeting ended and had ignored his text messages. Much like she was ignoring his end-of-shift radio pages.

Maybe she was avoiding him because she was afraid he'd be angry over her sharp parting shot. Maybe it was a measure of self-preservation. Either way, he wasn't mad—she had a right to call him out on his flaws, and he got her need to protect herself. It only left him more determined to prove that he loved her and wanted to try for a solution. They both needed to figure out how to have a balanced perspective on their hometown. He wasn't the only one who had a messed-up tie to the town. Lauren wanting to help her family was one thing. Being petrified to leave home was another. And her eyes had snapped with real fear yesterday.

Pressing the push-to-talk button, he repeated his page. She was scheduled to be doing safety checks at the river-rafting base camp, well within transmission range. He leaned back in his seat, picking up the list Lauren had left taped to Zach's computer screen. Back when they were married he might have called it a honey-do list, but they hadn't been married long enough to get into the habit of her making him lists and him pretending to complain about it.

The domestic picture made him smile, even though they weren't even close to finding that together. His efforts to chip away at his issues with Sutter Creek hadn't been enough for her so far—her rejection last night had made that more than clear. Had left him feeling emptier than he knew possible. The desolate look on her face had been enough to make him want to start digging a trench in her front yard. Prove he wasn't going anywhere, even if he couldn't believe he had that in him. Of course, she would have made it easier to tell her all of this had she picked up her phone one of the ten times he'd called her since she fled, leaving him with a pot full of spaghetti sauce and a heart full of regret.

About thirty seconds passed by before his radio crackled. "Lauren Dawson here. Is that you, Tavish?"

"Yeah. Uh, this is an open channel, but your cell seems to be off. Would you meet me for dinner at the hotel lounge?" Time to step up further. If she could show him a little patience, he'd be willing to go for a longer trial period.

The radio sat silent for way too long. After she'd given him enough time to knit a sweater, she replied, "I'll see you at six."

He heard every second tick by on his watch until it finally read six o'clock. He arrived at the lounge early, having gone home to shower and change into a pair of dark jeans and a checked dress shirt. Settling into one of the wing-backed chairs at a table for two, he studied one of the deer-horn-chic chandeliers.

The minute Lauren walked into the room wearing a casual, swirly, hot-sauce-red dress, his heart stopped.

"Look what you're missing," the dress screamed.

Message received, Dr. Dawson.

Heads turned as she traveled through the room. He stood and pulled out her chair.

"Tavish." She sat and crossed her legs. "Thought we covered everything we needed to last night."

"We covered it. But we didn't make any decisions. You ran off after making some awfully hypocritical claims." He tried to look her in the eye but she kept her gaze on her water glass as he sat. "As if I'm the only one who's committed to my job at the expense of our relationship."

Squaring her shoulders, her eyes snapped. "You have five minutes to convince me I want to order something for dinner."

No guarantee she'd stay even if he managed an argument worthy of one of his mother's closing statements. Better to make his point in the limited time she was giving him rather than wait and hope she'd let him buy her dinner. Unraveling the thick cloth napkin from his cutlery, he laid it over his lap. "You know, I never really think about it, but I guess you own part of this place, don't you?"

"Yes. Ten percent. Twenty-five of the new holistic health center that's opening next month." She glanced at her thin gold watch. "Four minutes, thirty-two seconds."

"And you're sure you enjoy being a doctor more than working for AlpinePeaks?"

Her eyes flashed. Not anger, though. Fear. "Medicine is me. And you're down to four minutes," she snapped, a poor attempt to cover up her obvious discomfort. She sank into her chair as if trying to blend with the navy-striped upholstery.

Impossible in that dress. Not that she needed to be wearing anything specific to stand out to him.

"The baby's the most important priority, and I fully intend to make my work schedule predictable," he said. "I'm willing to do a test run before the baby arrives, too. See how long I can stay in town before getting the urge to hop on a plane. I'll stay in town until I head for Phuket in the fall, and will come back when my contract is finished. We'll see where we stand. But I can't be the only one who gives, who sacrifices. You have to consider your choices, too."

Lauren blinked her mossy-gold eyes, the moisture in them almost forcing him to slide off the chair and fall to his knees. Her brow lowered and her lips pressed together. She sat there for a few seconds, staring at him hard enough to etch a laser dent in his forehead.

"And which of my choices would those be?" she bit out.

He pressed his lips together. She hadn't been willing to listen when he'd tried to argue that her dad and Cadie were grieving less than last year, so a different tack might be best. "I remember your mom being a compassionate woman, Laur. Had she lived, do you really think she'd have expected you to stick to a teenage dream?"

"It was her dream, too."

"Was it? Or was she just humoring what she likely thought was an in-the-moment passion?"

She covered her mouth, one hand crossed over the other, and let out a muffled, tearless sob.

The noise cut right through him. He was too far away to reach her, didn't know if she'd want him to anyway. "What do you need, Pixie?"

Squeezing her eyes shut, she fisted folds of the red fabric of her skirt. "I need to give those papers to my lawyer."

Wow. He'd gotten more than five minutes, but the answers he'd hoped she'd give eluded him. He'd hoped some more compromise on his part would prompt her to take even a tiny step toward him. Seemed he was out of luck there. What was it going to take to loosen the grip that Sutter Creek had on her?

Friday morning, Lauren got to the WiLA office early. She hadn't been able to sleep more than a sweaty patchwork of dreams and haze. Add in her pregnancy-induced craving for naps, and she was dragging her feet as she entered the office.

Yawning, she settled at her brother's desk and shifted papers around, staring at a few columns of numbers before recognizing her sleep-deprived uselessness. She'd screw up all her efforts to organize the winter first-aid inventory if she tried to do anything number-related. Instead, she opened a web browser on her brother's computer. Spending ten minutes getting caught up on royal family gossip was completely justified.

At 8:22 a.m., Tavish strolled in with his camera bag slung over a muscular shoulder. A pair of mirrored aviators managed to keep his hair sticking up only four, instead of six, ways to Sunday. Dark charcoal water splotches marked the gray cotton of his T-shirt and his khaki shorts looked to be completely soaked through.

Only his flip-flops looked dry. His smile was so wide it sucked all the administrative boring out of the room. She wished she could keep that level of energy in a jar for the days when life stole the grin from her face.

"Felt like a swim?" she asked.

He met her cocked brow with a sheepish smile. "I slipped on the edge of a bridge and ended up waist high in the creek."

"On which trail?" Clients taking headers into creeks wouldn't be the best for business.

"Summit."

She narrowed her eyes, no longer worried about people slipping and falling. "All the bridges on Summit have rails. And they were all intact yesterday."

"I might have been sitting on the railing." The corner of his mouth turned up. "It was the only way to get the right angle of a pair of dragonflies hovering over a rock in the middle of the creek."

"Did you wreck your camera?"

"I'm like a cat. I always land on my feet with my camera hand in the air." He demonstrated with an exaggerated pose.

"You are kind of catlike."

"Graceful?"

"Elusive."

A faint shadow crossed his face. "Ouch."

Heat splashed Lauren's cheeks and the back of her neck. "Sorry. Not what I meant."

"What did you mean?" Caution edged his tone.

"I was referring to your wanderlust, not your personality."

His earlier demeanor that had shone 120 watts of vibrancy into the room dimmed. "Right. Anyway, I need to ask a favor of you."

"Of course." Anything to make up for insulting him, for accusing him of being something he wasn't.

"I scratched myself. I was hoping you'd clean it up for me."

"Okay." Did her voice shake? *Please, no.*

Tavish looked at her funny.

Gah, her *okay* had for sure vibrated.

"You don't have to, Laur. I can go to the clinic."

She shook her head. "Of course I can do it."

"You sounded—"

"I'll do it," she insisted.

She led the way to the red-cross-labeled door at the end of the hall. Flicking on the light, she motioned him in. "Lie facedown on the cot."

The room suffocated her like a mouse hole. A stainless-steel counter and supply cabinets lined one wall; the cot, the other. Tavish settled himself along the length. Lauren glimpsed blood-soaked gauze and her stomach turned. She would love to blame morning sickness, but nope.

On his stomach, Tavish propped himself up on his elbows, straining the shoulders of his T-shirt. She snapped on a pair of gloves, would have preferred reacting to his hard muscles rather than his cut calf.

"I hope this habit of me being attacked by errant branches and you having to patch me up stops after today," he said.

"Me, too. Wouldn't want any more scars on you." Would prefer to never see his blood again, was more like it. She really hated…

No. You're fine. Swallowing, she slid a thick pad of sterile dressings under Tavish's calf to absorb the saline she planned to use to clean out whatever lay under his bandage.

She peeled back his makeshift dressing. Objectively, his cut wasn't bad. Through the lens of her nerves, though, she had to resist the impulse to dart from the room. "God, you're a bleeder."

"Yeah. Always makes it look worse than it is."

Whenever a real emergency hit, adrenaline kicked in, masked her fear. Times like this were what killed her—plenty bloody but lacking the life-or-death chemical surge.

Metallic saliva flooded her mouth. She clicked into automaton mode: clean, dry, dress. A bead of sweat trickled from her temple along her jaw.

"All done," she whispered. She grabbed his old dressing and the dirty under-padding. And she had no time to do anything except spin, aim for the sink and lose her breakfast.

Head hanging over the basin, forehead pressing against the cool metal tap, she turned on the water to wash away the evidence. She hadn't been uncontrollably sick from handling a wound since the first weeks of medical school. She'd trained herself not to react. Why had it changed?

Don't ask a question you don't want the answer to.

She glanced at Tavish and rested her forearms on the counter edge.

He sat straight-backed against the wall with mile-wide eyes. "Morning sickness?"

"Yeah."

His expression flattened. "You're lying."

"I'm not." She bit the edge off the *not.*

"Try again."

Lying required too much effort. "Blood makes me sick." She let that hang in the silence as she rinsed her mouth with water from the tap.

He stood and took her in a tight embrace. Her clammy forehead rested against the skin of his neck. His river-dampened clothing cooled the heat of embarrassment from her body.

"Does this usually happen when you're working?"

"No. I learned to control it. It's just come back over the last month or so."

"Because of the baby?"

She'd love to blame being pregnant, but couldn't bring herself to do it. "No. It's the stress of the partnership."

He exhaled through pursed lips. A faint whistle rode the stream of air. "Lauren."

The warning tone singed her pride. "I'm dealing with it."

"How?"

"I find the closest toilet." She smiled out her humiliation, pressed dry lips to his cotton-covered clavicle. "It's funny, you know…"

"I don't see you laughing," he murmured.

"Not funny ha-ha, funny hmm." Tracing her fingers through his hair, she said, "I've had thousands of good days in my life, yet it's the bad ones that have defined who I am."

"That's not unusual. I wouldn't be who I am today without my father having bolted." His words came out so matter-of-factly, she'd have missed his decades-old pain had she not been peering at his face.

"Exactly. And my mother's death clarified so much for me. Everyone started to say how much I was like her, and how tragic it had been that she'd died so young without really having been able to put her mark on the medical field…"

He sat down on the cot and pulled her onto his lap,

rubbing her bare knee with one rough hand. "Those two things aren't connected."

"Sure they are. That's what pushed me to become who I am."

"But it doesn't mean you can't change. If medicine doesn't make you happy, then you should try something else. You were going to give up the clinic to work internationally. Maybe you need to change fields entirely."

Her spine drew up. She met the encouragement in his gaze with what she hoped was confidence. "I can't just find a new career. Yeah, I was going to give up the clinic for the sake of our marriage. I'd convinced myself my mom would have been okay with that. But I was wrong."

"How can you be so sure?" His voice was so low she could barely hear it.

"I make a mark for her, Tavish." Working at the clinic, holding their family together—filling in the cracks that had formed when her mom had died.

He stroked a calming hand up to her shoulder blades. "You need to make a mark for you, not for everyone else."

"It's the same thing."

"There you go, lying again."

The murmured accusation sneaked under her skin. She squeezed her eyes shut, but not before moisture gathered at the corners. "I can't let my family down any more than I already have."

He wiped at her cheeks with the pad of his thumb. "Letting yourself down is the bigger crime."

He was making way too much sense. She hugged her rib cage. The vain attempt at shoring up her throbbing middle fell short. A cavernous ache spread from her chest into her limbs. "I can't be that selfish."

His arms stayed firm around her, as if he could sense how close she was to stumbling backward and curling into a ball on the cot. "Are you going to expect our child to be a doctor?"

"No." She pressed the pads of her thumbs against her eyes. "Of course not."

"So why would your mom—"

"I told you yesterday!" Her heartbeat raced. "It's about my expectations for me."

"Can't those adjust, Lauren? Parenthood's kinda the ultimate game changer."

"Are you finding it that way?" she retorted.

"Yeah, I am." Awe brightened his beautiful face. Acceptance and happiness she'd never expected from him. He'd made the commitment to stay for the summer and didn't seem to be regretting his decision at all. He'd proved he could change. So why couldn't she do the same?

She clamped down the thought. Tavish changing meant him trying to be a good father, a good partner. But the changes he was suggesting she make would be the opposite. Following him around the world would mean less stability for their child and would make it impossible for her to support her family. Scrunching up her face, she sighed, but it came out more like a wheeze.

He blanched and dropped his hand to her belly. "You feeling okay?"

"Baby-wise, yeah."

His obvious relief came out with a long breath. But he didn't take his hand away. Spreading his fingers low on her stomach, he kissed her forehead. "Never thought I'd hear myself saying this, but I'm so damn impatient for when I can feel our baby move inside you. To have you get so big that your bump gets in the way when I sneak a kiss."

Petals of pleasure—from the naked vulnerability he

showed, from the rush of joy of the intimate touch—
bloomed through her body. She settled her hand over
his, wanting to savor every second of having him connect with their child.

With her.

Her opportunities would be limited. And that sucked.
Only having him with her for six months of the year, dealing with weeks, months maybe, of Skyping and sleeping
next to an empty pillow, sounded miserable. But less miserable than having him sleeping in a separate apartment
when he was in town to visit their child. She didn't know
how to deal with him being away from her. Arranging
visitation, though, dropping off the baby at his apartment and going back to her big house alone... So much
worse. She couldn't meet him halfway when it came to
the clinic, to her family. So to compromise at all, she'd
have to learn to deal with missing him. To give him a
chance to leave and, like he'd said, trust him to return.
She made sure her smile tinted her tone when she said, "I
thought we'd agreed you weren't going to sneak kisses."

"No way can I stick by that promise," he growled.
With his hands on her waist, he spun her until she straddled his lap, groaning as she rolled her soft center against
his hardening length.

"No way would I want you to keep it." She cursed the
barrier of their shorts, layers of fabric keeping her from
blissful fulfillment. Bracing her hands on his rock-solid
shoulders, she closed her eyes and rolled her hips, wel-
coming the heat from the tantalizing friction of their
bodies.

Curving a hand under her ass, he dug his fingers into
the hair at her nape. His mouth singed the flesh over her
pulse as he laved the tender place. "This has gotta be for
more than a day, Lauren. I can't do more back-and-forth."

"Neither can I."

A deep groan rumbled from his lungs, vibrated against her ribs. "There'd better be a lock on this door. Wrap your legs around me."

She did. And he lifted her effortlessly, took a step forward. The snick of the dead bolt sounded, and then they were back on the cot and his fingers were scrabbling at the hem of her work polo. "I like you in teal," he said. "It brings out the green in your eyes. Makes me want to grab my camera." He lifted the shirt over her head and dropped it on the foot of the cot. Her bra followed suit. "But I like you better like this."

Cupping her breasts, he drew his tongue around one peaking nipple and then the other.

"Tease," she complained, pressing her fingertips into his upper arms as tantalizing pressure built at her core.

"Patience, please." He grazed his teeth on her nipple. Her breasts tightened under greedy pulls and sucks from his slick mouth. The rough-but-tender caresses of his hands coaxed a flood of desire through her body. It pooled in her veins, weighed down her limbs. But she had to touch him, too.

Two seconds of effort on her part had his shirt joining hers on the cot. "Lie down."

He stilled with his mouth over her breast. "Sorry?"

A gust of breath carried the word, cooling her wet nipple and sending shivers along her spine. "On your back. Lie down."

A raw flare lit his eyes and he obeyed, ripping off his sandals and sliding out of his shorts as he went. He was all hers, gold-shot, tousled hair on the white pillowcase, long body stretched out on the gray wool blanket. Beautiful, lean muscle and taut skin that she got to use for her own purposes. *For his pleasure.* He had thrown her off by kneeling in front of that picnic table the last time they were intimate. And she wasn't going to kneel—not today, anyway—but she was going to play.

Her shorts and shoes hit the floor, but she left her panties on. Her heart raced at the thought of him discovering how wet they'd become from having him kiss her breasts. Climbing on top of him, she lined up her swollen flesh over the ridge of his sex. Way fewer clothes between them without their shorts on, but even her panties and his boxers were too much.

Resting her hands on his abdomen, she played slow, silent piano over the cut ridges. "You took unapologetic advantage of my emotional state the other night. Had me like putty in your hands." She smirked at him to make sure he knew any advantage was freely given. "Question is, can I torture you into a similar state?"

"You can, Pixie. Anytime you want. Except..." He took her hands off his belly and brought them to his mouth, worshiping her palms with his lips. "I want to love you right this time."

He tugged on her arms, and she collapsed on his chest. Inhaling deeply, she filled her nose with his sultry, masculine scent. Bliss. "I don't remember complaining. If anything, I got the better deal."

"I disagree." She heard his smile. "Making you fall apart is about the best thing I get to do in life."

So why on earth was he so insistent that being around her all the time was such a problem? She checked the thought. It wasn't being around her; it was being around home. Hopefully his staying for half the year would be enough for both of them.

Rucking a hand into her hair, he flipped her gently onto her back, hovering over her with all his delicious bulk, his eyes smoky with need. "This is more what I had in mind."

"You on top?"

"No, you in my arms."

She melted at that, at his tender kiss. Their mouths fused, nipping and licking and tasting. He had both her panties and his underwear off in less than a blink of an eye.

With his weight on one arm and that hand tangled in her hair, he slid his other palm down the center of her torso until his fingers dipped over the bud of her arousal. "How'd you get so wet?"

It was probably pregnancy hormones in part, but mostly him. "You're good at this." She tilted one side of her mouth and reached to stroke his erection.

He released a groan so loud she shushed him—they were at work, after all—but she kept moving her hand, savoring velvet skin over rigid shaft.

He froze in place, his hand cupping her mound. She ached for the smallest movement. She twisted against his hand as she continued a slow rhythm with her own.

"I—Lauren. *Please.*"

"Please stop? Please more?"

"Please *you.*" He shuddered back to life and slipped his fingers down farther, into her. Her center clenched, begging him for more. "This."

She nudged him, guiding his body over hers, and his hips between her thighs until he was fully seated and they were both panting.

It was too much. Too good.

Too good to be true?

Wrapping her legs around his powerful hips, she silenced the thought and rode the ecstasy until her mind was blank.

Chapter Twelve

Satisfaction ebbed and flowed in Lauren's limbs. Tavish's chest warranted the award for best pillow in Montana. But responsibility tugged her out of the hazy wonder of the smell of their pleasure lingering in the air and the warmth of their bare skin where it touched. They could only hide in the first-aid room for so long before someone came looking for them. "We need to get back to work."

"Right. We're at work." He made a self-deprecating noise. "Classy."

"Oh, as if we're the only people who ended up using this cot for…personal shenanigans."

"Not sure if that makes it better," he murmured into her hair. "We're off tomorrow. We could spend the whole day somewhere way more romantic."

"We should take my canoe out."

He winced melodramatically and bent his leg, laying

a hand over the bandage. "Too wounded. The only cure's rest. Naked rest. Write me a prescription."

She pressed her lips to his delicious chest to muffle her giggle. "Take two orgasms and call me in the morning?"

"If I'm lucky." His tone turned reluctant, and he peeled himself away from her to get dressed.

She followed suit, wondering if he was as saddened to see her fasten her shorts as she was by him pulling his shirt over his head, covering up the delightful six-pack she almost had mapped with her fingers. She'd need to work on committing it fully to memory later. "Is your leg bothering you?"

"Stings, but nothing serious. I had a pretty thorough doctor."

She chewed on the inside of her lip. "I should make sure you're not under my care anymore, though. Not if we're together again. Ethics and all that."

"Ethics?" He blinked as if his thoughts were coming too quickly to process. "What about ethics and your other patients? Not in the sense of relationships," he said in a rush. "But when it comes to your fear of blood."

Looking up, she caught something in his expression that shot fear to her core. She crossed her legs on the cot and toyed with the clips on her hiking sandals. "I'm sorry?"

He settled next to her and laid a hand on her crossed ankles. "Will you always be able to guarantee that your duty to your job is going to be enough to make you a dedicated doctor? What if you stick with it for the sake of obligation, and then get to a point where your phobia impedes your ability to care for your patients?"

"My *phobia*?" Coming from him, the label felt like a wrecking ball crashing through the tower of reasons she'd created to stick with her job. Her hands started to shake and she grabbed handfuls of the scratchy gray blanket to steady them.

"Lauren. You get physically sick at the sight of blood. I'm not the medical professional here, but how is that not the definition of a phobia?"

Her lips parted but she couldn't get any sound out.

She'd been so focused on herself and on her belief she *wouldn't* fail, she hadn't truly processed the consequences of what would happen if she *did*. And he was right: given her recent inability to control her phobia— she had to be factual and start calling it that—it might at some point stop her from doing her best job. Might put a patient in harm's way, or prevent her from providing the best care possible. Prioritizing her desire to be like her mother over patient health went against everything she'd sworn upon completion of her medical degree. Her patients had to take precedence.

She gripped his hand with both of hers and let the truth sink from her brain to her heart to each cell of her body. It wasn't just the partnership that was the problem, it was medicine entirely. "Maybe I could go talk to someone about it. Get some therapy."

He traced a small circle on the back of her hand with his thumb. "Do you want to do that?"

"No." She looked into his eyes and repeated the realization with more emphasis. "No. I—I love having a career that helps people. That's something I'm always going to want. But being a doctor was never about me. And you're right, I can't risk harming a patient."

He stared at her with enough love to fill the inside of Sutter Mountain. "If you're worried about losing your mom in some way if you quit…you won't. The fact you and Drew and Cadie exist is enough of a legacy." He cleared his throat. "*Our* baby is a legacy."

Toying with the sprinkle of golden hair at his wrist, she said, "You're getting rather psychoanalytical there, but you're right." Holy crap, was she doing this? "I have to quit."

Disbelief cascaded through her. *Yup, doing this.*

He enveloped her, a perfect sum of strong muscles, fresh, air-scented cotton and genuine support. "Proud of you, Pixie."

Nice to know, but would her dad feel the same? Also, Frank was a good family friend and was going to be shocked as anything. And changing careers while pregnant... *Oh, my God.* She pressed a palm to her shaky stomach. "I need a minute. Alone."

"Sure." With tender lips, he brushed her cheek. Brought warmth back to her goose-bumped skin. Unlocking the door and swinging it open, he disappeared into the hallway.

Resisting the temptation to bury her face in the thin, medical-issue pillow on the cot, she stood and remade the bed with fresh sheets and blankets from the supply cupboard. Then she attacked the sink and counter with disinfectant. Trying to scrub her worries onto the stainless steel didn't work worth a damn.

With nothing else to clean, she headed for the office, numb and in a daze. Who would she be if not a doctor? What the hell would she do with herself?

"Lauren!"

She jumped at the blur of sunshine-yellow movement across the room.

Zach Cardenas sat at his desk, crutches leaning next to him. The color of his moisture-wicking T-shirt was almost as cheery as his expression. Lauren's pile of order forms fluttered in his hand. "These look good. You're a natural."

Not enough that she saw herself working for her brother as a career... Her gut clenched, and she hid her uncertainty behind a forced smile. "Zach. What are you doing here? Andrew told me you weren't back for weeks."

"Yeah, that was his opinion. Wanted me to focus entirely on my rehab. But I'm bored as hell at home. No reason I can't come do paperwork."

She collapsed into her brother's chair. Having the extra help for the next week would be nice if it wouldn't set back Zach's recovery. And having Zach's problems fall in her lap as a distraction from calling her dad counted as the best timing of the day. "Did you talk to Andrew about it, or are you using him being on holidays to sneak in unnoticed?"

He cringed, emphasizing the squareness of his handsome jaw. "More column B."

Lauren tsked. "And your therapist gave you the okay? Andrew said something about you being on skis this winter being more important than you working during the summer."

"As long as I limit my hours, I'm okay to put some work in." His face fell. "I can't stand sitting on my butt with nothing to do. I'll be able to work a half day and put in enough hours of physio and swimming and stationary biking to be healthy by October. I know it."

Tavish appeared in the doorway. "Zach. G'morning."

Zach gave him a cursory nod. His gaze lingered on Tavish's shirt. *Oh, crap.* He'd put it on inside out.

"I think if you can take more time off, you should take it," Lauren said, trying to distract Andrew's assistant from deciphering what she'd been doing with her ex-husband while technically on the clock. "I have things under control."

Zach smacked his palm against his desk. Lauren

jumped, along with Tavish. "I've been living off your dad's generosity for long enough."

Tavish started to sift through a tangle of carabiners on a far shelf. "Drew's going to be pissed if you come back early. I'm not going anywhere. I can keep filling in for you."

Yet another confirmation that Tavish intended to stick to his promise of staying around for the summer... It soothed like aloe vera on a sunburn. More solid, more real, more a guarantee rather than a desperate wish.

Zach grimaced. "Yeah, tell you what. Don't tell Dawson I'm back, and I'll take all the flack when he inevitably loses it. So fill me in. What've you guys been up to for the last week?"

Lauren and Tavish spent a full half hour answering Zach's multitude of questions concerning work.

"Have you guys taken any time to breathe since the wedding?" Zach asked.

"No," she said in sync with Tavish's, "Nope."

Zach glanced between them. "You should take the rest of today, then. I'll hold down the office, and I'll get Garnet to stand in as field supervisor."

"But we already have the weekend off," Lauren protested. "I like being busy."

It gave her an excuse not to quit her job or to call her dad right away.

"Don't listen to her," Tavish said. "We'd love the extra time. We could get out of town for a couple of nights. Go for a canoe in Yellowstone, maybe."

"Yellowstone," she croaked, a fist slowly clamping around her windpipe.

Tavish glanced at her, gaze evaluating. "Never mind. We'll stay local."

Zach looked at them funny. "What's the excitement in that?"

"Well, you might need us," she fudged.

Reaching over, Tavish covered her clasped hands. "And Moosehorn's good enough."

She let out a shaky breath. Yellowstone wasn't that far. But still. She hadn't been farther than Bozeman since she returned from Vegas. The idea of crossing state lines, the possibility that something could happen to her family while she was gone, made it feel like the marrow was shrinking in her bones.

"No one will need us if we take off for an overnight," Tavish promised. "But we can hold off on that."

"Or go. We'll be fine without you," Zach agreed, no doubt assuming Tavish meant something at work.

He didn't. She got the message, loud as a cracking avalanche. But for some reason he was giving her a pass, even though he thought she was irrational for being afraid to leave her family. Respecting the need for baby steps, maybe?

Baby. Right. She closed her eyes. She didn't have time to dawdle. She needed to address the paranoia she'd developed when her mom died. She'd challenged it once. Had completed her residency in Billings, then headed for Las Vegas. And her grandparents had been in their car accident. Not being able to say goodbye to Grammy, or to stand at her dad's side when he'd decided to have the ventilator unplugged had been unbearable. She didn't think she was responsible for any of her family members' deaths. But she'd always considered herself responsible for not having been able to support her dad and her siblings.

And she could no longer pretend she was acting like a healthy person.

Her breath hitched as her heart started to gallop. Only one way to move forward. After hitting the water with Tavish, she'd assemble the dregs of her courage, talk to her dad and go quit her job.

The only thing quieter than being out on the lake was being out on the lake with Lauren. Tavish was happy to enjoy the rustle of the wind in the trees and the slap of water against the canoe and their paddles without conversation. But he'd been staring at her back for over an hour and her shoulders looked tight enough to use as a springboard. Made him feel guilty for appreciating the stretchy mauve fabric shifting across her upper back as she paddled in the front seat. One of those built-in-bra, yoga situations that were invented to torture people who made a study of the female form. The shirt exposed tantalizing triangles of skin. The streamlined lifejacket she wore did little to cover up her sexy shoulders. He'd spent a good portion of their expedition plotting a route of the freckles he planned to kiss.

As much as his groin loved the view, the coffee and toast he'd had for breakfast churned in his stomach whenever his mind drifted to their earlier conversation. She'd made some major decisions today. And, yeah, he truly believed her quitting would make her happier. But would their compromises, their attempts to cobble together a life, make her happy, too? Being home this time felt different, for sure. Almost…right.

An aftershock of disbelief rolled through him, and he exhaled into a firm paddle stroke. Home had never *been* right, but he liked that it was starting to feel that way. Hope glimmered, a promise he'd be able to be the man Lauren and the baby deserved.

The midday sun glinted off her blond ponytail. Had

he been able to reach it he'd have tugged it to get her attention. "Keep it down up there. You're drowning out the birds."

She laid her paddle across her lap and scratched the back of her head with her middle finger.

"Aw. The romance is overwhelming, sweetheart."

Her other middle finger joined the first, the pair of profane gestures framing her ponytail.

He adjusted the angle of his paddle to make sure they didn't veer off course with her taking a break from her steady strokes. "Want to talk about it?"

"It's more a matter of doing it, Tav." Her brief over-the-shoulder glance gave him a glimpse of her pale skin and stress-widened eyes.

"*It* meaning...?"

"Going in and talking to Frank. And my dad. I should do it this afternoon. But I think I might need to give myself a day." With a wide grip, she clutched her paddle.

He flicked a small spray of water at her right arm. "You're going to break that shaft if you don't ease up."

Shaking the droplets of lake water from her forearm, she pivoted on her seat, bringing her feet around and facing him. She slid her paddle under the bow thwart and let go. It landed in the bottom of the canoe with a *thunk*. Twisting her hands in her lap for a few seconds, she made a face and then held on to the gunwales, tapping her fingers against the fiberglass hull. "One could say I'm having a hard time relaxing."

"Noticed that." He stilled his strokes and let the boat glide. Wanting to get a smile on her face, or at least earn a protest, he positioned the blade of his paddle over the water in an obvious I'm-going-to-spray-you angle.

"Peril awaits down that trail, Fitzgerald."

He raised a teasing eyebrow. "Peril?"

"Of the worst sort."

Resuming his stroke rhythm, he grinned. "Then I'll have to behave. I need a replay of our morning mischief." She smiled back, dipped her cupped hand in the water and showered him in the face, chilling his skin. "You need to cool off."

He dragged the back of his hand across the rivulets dripping from his jaw to his T-shirt. "Good aim." Though she'd thrown a lot more at him lately than just a palmful of lake water. "Would you rather head for shore and go deal with it? Then we'd have the rest of the weekend to relax."

The shake of her head sent her ponytail swaying. "I'll talk to Frank tomorrow morning. He usually does paperwork for a few hours on Saturday before he heads off golfing."

"What about your family?"

She blinked long, as if her indecision was weighing down her eyelids. "Soon."

Soon. Talk about a word that defined his life. Soon he'd be spending the winter in Sutter Creek. Soon Lauren would start to show.

Soon they'd be a family of three.

If living together for half the year counted as being a family. Tension gripped his chest. After they'd tried him being home for a few months, he could reassess. Rubbing his palm against his aching sternum, he sent her a lopsided smile. "Uh, speaking of telling people things—when are we going to make our sprout public knowledge?"

The birds on the shore had enough time to sing a symphony as she chewed on her lip. "Three months is pretty usual, and I'm eight weeks along by medical standards. Though Cadie already knows."

He tried not to narrow his eyes, but alarm bells rang in his skull. "I'd like to at least tell our parents."

"I'd like to wait."

"Why?"

"It's still early." Her voice went achingly quiet. "I could miscarry."

Miscarry. His throat closed over and he had to cough. "Yeah, but… Would it be so bad if our families knew about a miscarriage?"

By the way she stared at the tree line, pine boughs must have become the most fascinating view on the planet. When she finally looked at him, the green in her irises had swallowed any golden light. "If I miscarried, would you still stay?"

"I—" Would he? The baby had been the push to get him to commit to living at home half time, but… "Lauren. I'm staying for you just as much as the baby."

"Right." She dropped her gaze to her knees.

Which was a relief because the lack of trust on her face made him feel like he was hanging from the Peak Chair by his fingernails.

Time. Time would convince her. And could maybe help her see that he was stepping out on an emotional limb, too. "You know, you aren't the only person who's been hurt in this relationship. The first time we broke up, you were the one who cut and ran."

She made a dismissive noise. "A high school break-up is on a different continent from a divorce."

"Tell that to my nineteen-year-old self. I was devastated."

His words came out soft, but by the way her face crumbled, she hadn't missed a syllable. "Maybe there's too much bad history between us to make this work."

"Not if we decide to move beyond our past." The six or

so feet separating them was too much to handle. Leaving his paddle next to Lauren's, he crouched low. He held on to the sides of the canoe and maneuvered forward, then sat on the metal bow thwart and braced his knees against the fiberglass sides. He took her hands in his. Jesus, they were cold. And not just the one she'd dipped in the lake.

Her gaze dipped to his makeshift seat. "You're too heavy to sit there. You'll break the canoe."

"I'm more worried about making sure I don't break your heart."

By the next morning Lauren wished she'd taken Tavish up on his advice to talk to Frank and her dad yesterday. As she walked into the clinic and waved at the reception-ist, she smothered a yawn. She'd be in a better head space had she not spent the night fretfully tossing and turning.

She headed for Frank's office before she turned on a heel and went back to her car. Three deep breaths in the corridor filled her with just enough courage to step over the threshold.

Her boss, in his usual work outfit of a lab coat over a plaid dress shirt, removed his reading glasses and slid them into the breast pocket of his white coat. He tilted his head. "You don't look rested for someone who's been on holidays for two weeks."

"Yeah. I didn't sleep well." Declining his nodded in-vitation to sit, she handed him the envelope stuffed with unsigned contract papers. "I need to give you the con-tract back."

"Finally." With an outstretched hand, he took the doc-ument and shot her a satisfied smile.

All the blood in her body rushed to her head, thunder-ing like a summer storm. "I didn't sign it."

He froze, but for his open, no-longer-smiling mouth and one raised, gray-speckled eyebrow. "What?"

Hands sweaty, she fiddled with the embroidered hem of her cap-sleeve blouse. "No. I'm afraid I'm going to have to give my notice. I need to…to pursue other options."

He laid the packet on his desk blotter and sat back, linking his fingers behind his head. "I'm confused, Lauren."

"I'll bet. I am, too, really. But I've come to realize medicine isn't as fulfilling as I'd hoped it would be. And it's too important to only commit to halfheartedly. Which precludes me from becoming a partner, or from working here in a different capacity."

He blew out a short burst of air. "Wow. I didn't expect this."

"I hope it won't be overly difficult to replace me."

"It's less about struggling to find someone and more about not wanting to have to."

She winced.

"I expect you'll be able to work for the four weeks' notice in your existing contract?"

"Yes, of course. Though I've been dealing with some, uh, queasiness lately. Might I ask to steer clear of suturing?"

"We can arrange that." He paused, calculation whirring on his face. "And if any other health or family issues are playing into your decision, know that we can adjust for that, too."

She shook her head. "To be blunt, I can't keep trying to bring my mom back by trying to be her, Frank. I need to live for me." And saying that out loud to someone other than Tavish released a buildup of pressure in her chest. Her body tingled as a sense of rightness filled her. After an awkward goodbye, Lauren headed for her car. Come mid-August, she would be free. Free to… Who knew?

Panic flooded her veins. Her polite-society vocabulary dissolved, leaving behind a selection of expletives more suited to a hockey locker room. Crawling behind the wheel, she let a few of them fly.

Her single-minded focus on medicine left her with a minimal grasp on what her other career-oriented aptitudes were. Money wasn't an issue—her savings and her AlpinePeaks profit share would provide for her and the baby for a long while. But she wasn't satisfied with the idea of doing nothing. Maybe she could explore a position at the new holistic health center. She could pitch in more with the opening, see if there was some sort of health management position she'd be suited to.

The possibility of working for one of the family businesses, working with Cadie, no less, took away some of the sting of quitting. Plus, long-term commitments elsewhere would be tricky with her going on maternity leave in eight months.

Holy crap. I'm actually changing careers. Something her dad should find out from her, not the Sutter Creek grapevine.

Going to see him in person would be the right thing to do, but after facing Frank, she was out of backbone. Shame rolled in her stomach as she pulled up her dad's number on her cell, but her lungs loosened, finally allowing a full breath. She wouldn't have to look at him when she let him down.

Giving her notice and admitting to Frank that she'd entered medicine for the wrong reasons had been easy compared to this. She itched to press the disconnect button.

He answered after two rings. "Hey, Cookie. What's shaking?"

"Oh, I dunno, Dad." *My voice, for one.* She drew in

air, tried to bring her pitch down a half octave. "Got a minute?"

"I'm all ears." Alarm erased his previously cheerful tone.

"I've quit my job."

Silence.

A load of it.

"You what?" he said.

She clicked over to her hands-free device and took her time explaining her phobia, the expectations she'd always felt from him and her family, and how she'd felt she needed to make up for her mom's shortened life.

More silence.

A lump filled her throat. She barely forced out her question. "You still there, Dad?"

"I'm here." He coughed. "Just give me a few seconds to process."

The few seconds clicked by slower than a year. "Um, want to tell me what you're thinking?" She didn't really want to know, but might as well rip off the proverbial Band-Aid.

"I'm...shocked. Confused about what you'll do with yourself. Not to mention feeling guilty for so often having compared you to your mother. Why didn't you tell me how much pressure that put on you?"

"I was scared," she whispered. She could picture him sitting palm to forehead, elbow on the edge of his desk, as he often did when thinking.

"I'm sorry, Lauren." The rough regret in his voice scraped against her skin.

"Don't be sorry. For as much as I don't want to be a doctor, I—I liked being close to Mom."

Slow breathing filled the speaker. "I'm feeling pretty thrown here, Cookie. Can you do something for me?"

"Sure, Dad. Anything."

"Get some space, some time away by yourself—you need to think about what you'll do next, and you're too busy when you're at home."

He wanted her to leave? Her stomach twisted. Before her morning sickness could take over, she cut their call short and dropped her forehead to the steering wheel. After a minute or so, her nausea settled. She started driving down streets she'd traveled thousands of times, didn't really need to see to safely pilot the vehicle. The familiarity left her brain with way too much freedom to stew over her conversation with her father. Did he want her to get away from town? From Tavish? From their family?

Gah.

Maybe her dad was right. And Tavish, too, about her family not falling apart if she went away for a weekend. Her brain threatened to overflow; clearing it sounded like a brilliant plan.

A few minutes later she knocked on Tavish's apartment door.

A moment passed before it swung open. And wow, that moment had been worth the wait. A pair of green-striped boxers hugged his hips, right below the V of hard muscle that pointed straight to a tempting, cotton-covered bulge. Most of him was on display. Delineated biceps and powerful thighs and a drowsy grin. "Hey, Pixie."

Her heart warmed at the endearment. "Hey, yourself, sleepyhead."

She walked into his embrace. He smelled like clean sheets and warm man. The anchor of his rock-hard arm muscles around her adrenaline-wearied body was everything she'd needed since she'd walked into Frank Martin's office. Her mouth met his, kissed away the trace of chap on his lower lip. "Let's go somewhere. Together."

His eyes opened wider, lost some of their just-wakened cloud. "Where?"

"Yellowstone." She tugged on one of the buttons of her blouse and threaded the fingers of her other hand into the crispy hair above the waist of his boxers. "But first, I'm taking you back to bed."

Hours later, body sated, she snuggled under the thin feather duvet. A clatter rang through the open bedroom door, followed by a soft curse from Tavish.

"Whatcha doing?" she called.

He came back into the room, holding a flat, brown-paper-wrapped package under his left arm. He looked ready to attack the wilderness in beige nylon cargo shorts, a threadbare Sutter Creek Canoe and Kayak Club T-shirt and a pair of hiking sandals. Her heart fluttered—part anxiety, part anticipation—at the possibilities.

"Unwrap this." His shoulders slumped a fraction and he ran a hand through his hair.

She sat up with the sheet tucked under her armpits and took the gift, tearing off the paper.

Framed with matting colors of sage and cream, his river drawing looked even more real than when she'd last seen it in the office. Choking on the tears clogging her throat, she whispered, "Your sketch..."

"It'll match your living room. If you want it in there, of course. No obligation."

"It's perfect."

He brushed his fingers along her arm. "I was thinking of you when I drew it. It just seemed right to give it to you."

"It was a big place in our life."

"Yeah. Beginnings." He sighed. "Endings. Uh, the tattoo on my side is all about you, too."

Oh. *Oh*. She'd wondered about the connection. God,

if she was looking for proof of how deeply his feelings ran, she couldn't get much more than him permanently inking the memory of their love on his skin. She kissed him softly. "Thank you."

After drawing her further in, turning the kiss long and hot and nerve-jarring, he said, "Let's go find more big places."

"Right. Gear all packed?"

"Let's get gone."

She pressed a hand to her chest. Could she do this? Fully face her fears? Yes or no, she was going to try.

Chapter Thirteen

Tavish's mouth watered as his feet crunched on the rock-strewn path. Nothing on the Grebe Lake trail could hold a candle to watching Lauren's hamstrings tense and release. Every once in a while she'd turn to smile at him, her metallic-green, oversize sunglasses making her look like a June bug. And the activity had brought the color back into her cheeks. About time. When he'd driven across the Montana-Wyoming border, she'd gone sheet-white.

Curiosity ate at him to find out what had happened when she'd spoken with Frank Martin and her dad, but she hadn't wanted to talk about it when he'd prodded.

He'd wait.

And would watch her legs in the meantime.

When they got to the lake's edge, she shed her socks and shoes and immediately headed for the water. Knee-deep, she turned around and grinned. Her obvious delight filled his chest to bursting, making him feel like he'd won a Pulitzer. And when she lifted the bottom edge of her athletic tank to drag the sheen off her face, his tongue begged him to drop to his knees, to lick the exposed inches of her pale stomach. Was he crazy, or was there a little fullness around her waist that hadn't been there a week ago?

"You look hungry, Fitzgerald." A smile played on her lips.

"I am."

"Well, I'm not on the menu. Yet." Her smile turned to a full-on grin. "Make me lunch. Your kid needs to be fed."

My kid. Wow. But he was getting used to the phrase. Damn attached to it, really.

They settled in on a sandy, secluded stretch of lakefront and unpacked their hastily gathered picnic from his day pack.

Lauren reclined against a log, shoes off and knees bent. Her tanned calves matched the golden-brown sand that caked her feet after her wade in the lake.

A palm-size cluster of condensation-frosted grapes dangled between her forefinger and thumb. She sucked the juicy buds of fruit from the stem. Plump lips enveloped a grape and then, with a pop, disappeared, along with Tavish's hold on his lust. He wanted her to suck his skin in that same methodical way.

Not in the mood for exhibitionism, he reached for food instead. There was no guarantee they wouldn't be interrupted by other hikers.

She shot him a sly, sexy smile.

Then sucked.

Grape. Grape. Fingertip.

Lust burned his skin and he swallowed. "You prepared to follow up on that smile, Dr. Dawson?"

Her mouth gaped, playful mood vanishing from her face and posture. "I won't be a practicing doctor for much longer. Weird."

Way to go, Fitzgerald. He'd been so careful not to mention work. "Weird in a good way?"

"Yeah, I think so."

"We don't have to talk about it."

"I'm ready."

He listened intently to her explanation of her resignation and talking to her dad. She'd done swift work, untangling herself from her job. And with no longer being attached to the clinic, would she change her mind about traveling with him when he worked? Something else to find out when the time was right.

He shifted to sit next to her and ringed his arms around her shoulders. Dropping a kiss on her head, he said, "That can't have been easy."

"It wasn't."

"I have something to tell you, too. I haven't signed off on anything, but that job at Montana State I called about? I've been offered an artist-in-residence position for January. I can't start until then because of the few contracts I have for the fall, but I thought I'd give it a shot."

She gripped one of his knees and looked at him, solemn, doubtful. "You sure you want to do that?"

"I'm sure I want you, Lauren. I'll do my best."

"I don't want you to make yourself miserable for me. Or the baby."

Tavish nuzzled her neck. An outdoor lake-and-flora smell, the one fabric softener manufacturers spent millions trying to reproduce but never came close to, clung to her skin. "I've been pretty miserable without you. And no way do I want to miss out on watching you growing our baby this winter." He didn't know when the urge to leave would kick in. Given he was his father's son, it would hit him eventually. Because of that, he wasn't going to promise forever. But he could promise his best. He'd *always* give his child—and the woman he'd created that child with—his best. Hopefully it would be good enough.

He spread his fingers across her stomach. Incredible that the beginnings of a human dwelled safe inside her. "I love you, Lauren. And I figure it's worth doing what I can to see if that love can survive. I want to be connected to you beyond parenting together. And we're both closer to finding middle ground. You're here with me today. Maybe you'd travel with me again before the baby's born. Phuket has some nice resorts. We could stay on a few weeks after I'm done my assignment in the fall. Chill out on a pair of beach chairs—what do people call it, a babymoon?"

"Tavish." The ache in her voice pulled at any sense of hope he was attempting to generate. She shook her head. "Being willing to go on an overnight camping trip a few hours from home is a heck of a lot different than going to Thailand for a month. I *just* quit, for God's sake. I won't be able to take a vacation if I'm figuring out a new job."

He sighed. "You'll get vacation time, Lauren, so be honest—it's the home part that's holding you back. And given the world didn't fall down around your ears when we crossed into Yellowstone Park boundaries, you could probably safely get on a plane, too."

"Traveling halfway around the world is different from pitching a tent a couple of hours from home. This is too fast, too much pushing." She emphasized the last few words, making them echo across the lake.

He forced himself to suck in a calming breath. "We'll take it slow, then."

Her eyes shuttered and she let out a slow breath

through pursed lips. "We'll take a pause, you mean. This is enough for me for now."

A pause? Fine. Or so he'd convince himself.

Lauren woke up to the twitter of early-morning birds and insects. She squinted at the tent walls, lit cobalt in the shadows of the trees around their campsite. That dim, just-after-dawn light. Tavish's arm lay heavy across her rib cage, his breathing steady against her back.

Why was she awake?

A buzz sounded from inside her backpack. Ah, her phone was the culprit. Stupid social media alerts, going off at all hours even out in the wilderness.

All hours. Hours from home. An anxious tingle crawled through her abdomen. The scent of vinyl started to unsettle her stomach and she reached for her water bottle just as another buzz interrupted the silence, from the pocket of Tavish's hoodie this time.

Coincidence? Her heart started pounding as she rooted around for her cell. As she closed her hand around it, it went off again. She reared up from the mattress and looked at the screen.

"What's wrong, sweetheart?" Tavish murmured, voice raspy.

"Cadie's calling." Fear ripped through her as she answered. "Cadie? What's the matter?"

"I'm at th-the h-hospital in Bozeman…" Cadie stuttered, and not from bad phone reception. "Dad. A heart attack."

"No!" She fell back against Tavish, who swore under his breath and caught her in his embrace. Cadie's words blurred together. Something about surgery and wanting Lauren home.

"But I'm hours away!"

"Dad will be in surgery for a while anyway. Just come as fast as you can."

Guilt squeezed Lauren until the phone fell out of her hand. She curled into a ball in Tavish's arms. *This is my fault.* She'd left her family, and yet again something had gone wrong... She wasn't home for Cadie or her dad when they needed her. *Again.*

In a fog, she shook as Tavish picked up the phone and promised Cadie they'd be there as soon as they could.

"I shouldn't have come."

"Shh."

"They need me and I'm not there." Tears pricked her eyes. "What if he was stressed out about me quitting?"

"Hey." He squeezed her tight, but the comforting support only made her feel worse for not being at home, hugging her sister. "You didn't cause this in any way. Grab your backpack. I can have everything taken down in ten minutes."

Muscles weak, she dressed, stuffed her belongings into her pack and threw it in the vehicle. He yanked on yesterday night's sweats and long-sleeved T-shirt, grabbed his own bag, and let down the food he'd strung up in a tree. He had the fire out and the tent stowed away before she'd even managed to deal with their sleeping bags.

She tried to help further, but her fingers fumbled her tasks. Fear curdled her stomach, souring the back of her throat. She gave up and sat in the passenger seat, letting the tears come.

By the time Tavish shut the hatch and climbed into the driver's seat, her breath was coming in gasps and her diaphragm was starting to ache.

"Pixie. You need to get your breathing under control." He ran his thumb across one of her tear-slicked cheeks.

His eyes were a stormy violet-gray. "In and out, Laur. You can do this."

Pretending it was yoga class, she followed his instructions and managed to slow her sobs to irregular hiccups. "Start the car, Tavish."

"I want you to be calm first."

"I'll be calm when I see my dad alive and complaining in post-op."

Exhaling in clear frustration, he shook his head but started the vehicle. Her regret over giving in to selfishness, for having left town, haunted her for the first two hours of their drive.

A half hour from the hospital, Tavish, who'd—bless him—stayed mostly silent since leaving the campsite, gripped her hand and cleared his throat. "It's just a coincidence."

She pulled her fingers from his grasp. Crossing her arms around her already constricted ribs, she couldn't hold in her self-directed vitriol any longer. "Well, I'm sick of my coincidences hurting the people I love."

Tavish guided Lauren into the hospital waiting room, hand at the base of her palpably knotted neck. The pastel green walls matched her complexion. Her morning sickness had kicked in the minute they'd passed through the sliding doors into the lobby. She'd sprinted to a garbage can and puked up the granola bar he'd made her eat as they'd passed through West Yellowstone.

Cadie sat in one of the banks of institutional fabric chairs, clasping a sobbing Ben to her chest like a life preserver. A wet splotch marked the front of her gray hoodie.

Lauren fell into the chair next to Cadie. She hugged her sister and her nephew at the same time. "Here, let me take Ben." Lifting the baby, she kissed his tear-streaked cheeks. "Hey there, buddy. How 'bout you calm down for Auntie Lauren?"

The shudders gripping Ben's tiny body lessened then stopped.

Tavish sat next to Lauren and stared at her, awe spreading through him. Man, she was going to be a good mom. With any luck, she'd make up for his inevitable screwups. He'd spent some time around children on the job, but his learning curve would be mighty steep.

Relief softened the exhaustion lining Cadie's eyes. "Thanks. When I'm wound up, he won't settle."

"Any time." Lauren smoothed a hand over Ben's fine hair. "What's going on? Angioplasty? Bypass?"

"Angioplasty. Dad's in recovery—everything went fine. The surgeon said we should expect to be able to see him around nine."

"Oh, thank God. I don't know what I would have done..." Lauren shook her head and let out a huge breath in spurts. "Have you had breakfast?"

"No." Cadie looked apologetic. "I fed Ben, but not me. I don't think I could eat."

"Me neither," Lauren said.

Tavish reached around her and stroked the backs of two fingers along Ben's soft cheek. Soon it would be Lauren having, holding, soothing *their* baby. A thrill of possession shot up his spine. He could get used to the weight of her against his chest, her arms full of little boy. But the resurgence of her I-need-to-be-no-more-than-three-feet-away-from-my-family-at-all-times routine made him wary. Hopefully, once the initial panic over her father subsided, they'd be able to get back to her talking about travel. "Cadie, did you get a hold of Drew? We tried in the car but he wasn't answering."

Cadie nodded. "He and Mackenzie should be here soon."

"Andrew called me ten minutes ago," Zach Cardenas said as he arrived in the doorless archway. He leaned on his crutches. "They're almost here." His throat bobbed. "I'm so sorry, Cadence. I came to see if I can help in any way."

Cadie's face crumpled at the same time her eyes brightened. She jumped up and rushed to Zach, who leaned to his left and put his weight on his nonbraced leg. He wrapped her in his arms. One of his crutches fell to the floor. And as his eyes closed, his heart cracked clear across his face.

Tavish knew that look, knew that feeling. Knew his face was probably as obvious as Zach's.

"What do you need?" Zach asked.

"I don't know. Aunt Georgie's going to come as soon as she finishes all the morning chores out at the ranch, and I can't really ask her to babysit. But I want to take Ben home."

"I can do that," Zach said.

Cadie shook her tousled curls. "You're using crutches. Ben's too active for you."

"You have a stroller and a baby carrier. I won't have to lug him around all that much." Zach tipped Cadie's chin up. "I can handle Ben for a few hours. Garnet's got everything under control at the office."

"Okay. You can follow me home, then." She freed herself from Zach's arms and busied herself with taking a now-sleeping Ben from Lauren and transferring him to his stroller.

Lauren, shooting her sister an "I see what you did there, looking at that guy in that way" brow arch, slipped off her shoes, rested her heels on the edge of the chair and sank against Tavish. He absorbed her weight into his side and kissed her hair, which looked rather like she'd been standing in a windstorm. He wasn't about to point that out. "You should both eat something."

"I can't," Lauren said. "I won't keep it down."

"Your dad's going to be fine. And you need to think of yourself," Tavish emphasized. He lowered his voice to a whisper. "Think of the—"

"Fine." Her jaw jutted out. "But I'm not eating cafeteria crap."

"I can bring us something healthy from home," Cadie said. "Though that'll be well over an hour with driving."

"I'll survive," Lauren said.

As Cadie and Zach's footsteps—or crutch squeaks, in Zach's case—faded down the hallway, Lauren slid away from Tavish and dropped her head against the back of the chair. "Don't be so obvious. I'm not ready to announce my pregnancy to the world."

"But Cadie knows."

"And Zach doesn't."

"Sorry. I tried to whisper." Tavish's stomach gurgled. "I can't wait for breakfast—what can I get you from the cafeteria?"

Lauren nodded. "Tea, please. Green."

He headed for the elevator.

Alone in the waiting room, Lauren inhaled, gagging at the hospital smell. She didn't have much longer to deal with the smells of medicine—disinfectant, latex, bodily fluids. But her flash of happiness over that vanished when she remembered why she was in the hospital in the first place. Worry made the base of her throat tingle. *Dad will be okay.* Angioplasty rarely resulted in complications. She wasn't a cardiologist or a surgeon, but she knew enough.

Even so, her knowledge didn't stop the stress from corroding her stomach lining.

Tavish returned after ten minutes, holding a disposable tray, replete with cups and two muffins, in one hand.

"I brought you a muffin just in case." He sat next to her and kissed her softly. "Any news?"

He was being so attentive. But that didn't bring ease. In her under-slept, stressed state, her whole body buzzed, waiting for the rug pull. Waiting for him to bolt after her freak-out this morning. "No, no word yet."

"Come here." He welcomed her with arms she'd grown too used to over the last couple of weeks.

Sliding her legs over his lap, she clung to him, dug her fingers into the tense muscles of his shoulders. Even if her father's cardiac event meant she wouldn't be able to take any more steps forward, she needed Tavish's support. But if he kept pushing her like he had yesterday, their relationship wasn't going to go far. Were they better off giving up now, focusing on coparenting? No way was Lauren setting foot outside Gallatin County after she gave birth. Her baby needed a stable home. Safe. One where parents didn't get sick or die when their children weren't home.

Out on the trail yesterday, he'd smiled bright enough to give the sun a run for its money. Even the short distance had brought him joy. How much happier would he be had she been able to go farther? And she wouldn't be able to live with herself if she was the reason for that smile dimming again.

Unpleasant and unwanted, the truth hardened into a ball in her throat. She swallowed and made herself spit the words out before she convinced herself it was okay to keep holding him back. "You're not going to be happy in a relationship with someone like me, Tavish. Even part-time."

He jerked and a strange, still energy overtook his body. "We'll manage, Lauren."

No. Managing wasn't good enough. Wasn't fair for anyone. She couldn't expect Tavish to stay if she wasn't going to be able to compromise. "You should go."

"What?" He wove his fingers into her hair, held her head to his chest. His heart thudded against her ear. The physical comfort was the most unfair of teases. "I want to be here for you."

"I know you do. But you have needs, too. You deserve an equal partnership, someone who can meet you halfway. I thought I could do it, but I can't." She had to protect her heart as best she could. They had seven months to talk about sharing responsibility. She couldn't do seven more minutes with Tavish at her side, knowing she couldn't go with him when he left, couldn't be what he needed. Shifting her legs from his lap, she settled her feet on the floor. She gripped the edge of her seat and tried to muster strength. Alone.

"Lauren." His voice rasped, pain slicing into the sounds. "Give yourself some time. You've had a big shock—no need to make decisions right now. I think between me working at the college part-time and taking shorter assignments—"

"No. Part-time won't work."

"But…" The tendons and muscles of his hand slackened on her back. Then the comforting weight was gone. "You can't mean that."

Oh, she could. Yeah, she was hurting him, and she hated herself for it. But hanging on to something flawed and hurting him even more, keeping him in a relationship that would slowly make him miserable? She loved him too much to do that to him.

Shooting to his feet, he paced in a circle in front of her. He stuck his hands behind his head. The naked anguish in his eyes shredded her insides.

Tears welled, dripped onto her sweatshirt. "I love you. I can't ask you to compromise further, knowing it will make you unhappy."

"You want to talk about unhappy? *This* is making me unhappy, sweetheart. It's not right. I need you. And I want to be the man you need." His arms fell to his sides and he lingered in front of her for a minute or so, lips parted, silently begging.

"Just leave. Please." When she broke eye contact, unable to handle the violet bruise of his eyes any longer, he spun around. His footsteps receded.

Jarred by each reverberation of rubber against linoleum, Lauren's heart shattered.

Chapter Fourteen

Tavish stormed away from the waiting room. He'd done what Lauren had asked, but he didn't like it. The craving to stay with her, to hold her and wipe away her tears, overrode everything he'd ever wanted. That, he didn't know how to deal with. His instincts were all wonky. She was trying to leave him. He should be cutting and running first, saving himself the inevitable arterial bleed of having her break things off for good. Of her limiting their relationship to cold shoulders and stilted conversations on his visitation days. But his muscles resisted every step he took away from her. *I love you. I can't ask you...*

Alarm bells sounded in his mind. He stopped short, sandals screeching on the floor. She was pulling the exact same crap on him as he'd pulled on her when he'd left her sitting on the banks of the river. The classic "I love you so I'm going to push you away" garbage that had been his MO since he was a kid. Since his dad had left him.

Blinking away the moisture in his eyes, he clenched his hands into fists and straightened. *Try again, Pixie.* No way would he let her make the same mistakes he'd been making for most of his life. But who was he to show her how to love? He didn't even trust himself to commit to more than half a year with her and the baby.

Loving her—at least right now, while she was dealing with her dad's trauma—would require meeting her more than halfway. Sweat broke out on his palms and he slumped against one of the hallway walls. Could he do more than half a year? She clearly didn't trust him to, with her talking about him being unhappy. But he'd told her the absolute truth—leaving her was not right. Walking away while she sat alone in that uncomfortable hospital chair made him unhappier than staying in Sutter Creek ever had.

The mammoth task of convincing her to trust him weighed him down as if he were stuck under six feet of packed snow. Because before he could convince her to trust him, he had to learn how to trust himself.

And he didn't know where to start.

Weariness flooded into his muscles. More caffeine would jolt him back to reality. Having left his coffee behind, he needed to get another before he began the stake-out he intended to hold in the lobby on the main floor. He'd damn well sit there until he figured out how to show her that pushing him away was a stupid-ass way to express love.

He peeled himself off the wall and strode into the elevator. The smell of antiseptic and illness permeated the space and seeped into his pores. A shower would be nice, but he couldn't risk heading home and having her think he'd left. With a ding, the doors opened on the ground floor. Before he could exit, a couple rushed in, leaving him no room to squeeze out.

"Tavish!" His sister flung herself at him. Her freckles competed for space with the mottled blotches on her face. She'd always turned bright red when she cried.

"Kenz. Hey." He gripped her tighter. She felt rounder than she had a week ago. "You grew."

"Thanks for the reminder, jerk."

"It's a good thing," he assured her.

She snorted, obviously unconvinced. But he meant it. And excitement nudged away some of his irritation over Lauren's you-should-go nonsense. Pretty soon her body would start changing. He wanted it all, from feeling the baby kick to dealing with inevitable hormone swings. "You're not leaving, are you?" His shirt muffled Mackenzie's voice.

"No, I was going to get myself a coffee."

"How's my dad?" Drew's haggard expression broadcast his level of distress.

Tavish wished he had a father he could feel that depth of emotion for. "Recovering well. I'll take you to the waiting room."

As they rode back up to the cardiac floor, he filled the couple in on what he knew. The waiting room was empty—Lauren no longer sat where he'd left her. At the nurses' station, a guy in blue scrubs told them where to find Edward Dawson.

Drew held Mackenzie's hand as they hurried to the designated room. A nurse stopped them before they entered. "Sorry, you're going to have to limit it to one more visitor. He already has two."

"I should leave. Lauren doesn't want to see me anyway." Tavish backed up.

Mackenzie shot him a questioning look before standing on her toes to kiss her husband. "You go in, honey. I'll take a walk with my brother."

Drew's brow wrinkled. He clutched Mackenzie close. "If you're sure."

"We've been sitting for long enough. A stroll will do me good. Text me if you need me."

Nodding, Drew ducked into his father's room.

"Let's go somewhere happier," Mackenzie said.

Lauren sat at her father's bedside, her attempts to regulate her breathing a fricking failure. Illness came with the territory of her job. But her dad, pale and swathed in blue hospital linens and monitor cables was completely different. She could have lost him. God, she'd almost missed getting to tell him he was going to be a grandfather again. Her final memory of his voice could have been that quiet, shocked tone as he'd processed her having quit. Her eyes went hot.

Her aunt Georgie stood with Andrew against the wall. The two were talking quietly about the arrangements that needed to be made to get Edward some help at home and work for the next while. Lauren planned to ask Dr. Martin if she could take some family time, or at least cut her schedule down until her contract expired, to allow her to give her dad a hand.

"Laur, we're going to go make a few phone calls. We'll be quick," Andrew said.

"Sure," she murmured as her brother and her aunt left the room.

She traced her fingers along her father's wrist. Her father stirred.

"Daddy?"

He grimaced and then opened his eyes. "Cookie. Hey."

Her lower lip started to wobble. "Oh, Dad."

"Love you."

"I love you, too." Lauren squeezed his anesthesia-chilled hand. Hers wasn't much warmer, really. "Don't move, Dad. You're in the hospital. Do you remember what happened?"

"Yeah. Woke up. Four-thirty?" Swallowing, he glanced around the room without moving his head. He'd want water to moisten what had to be a surgery-munged mouth, but she couldn't let go of his hand just yet. "Crushing pain. Surgery."

Relief swamped Lauren at the sound of his voice, releasing the tears welling in her ducts. "I was so worried about you. But the surgeon said everything went fine."

"It's all pretty foggy."

She sniffled. "This is my fault. I stressed you out too much by quitting my job."

Her father's gaze sharpened. "Try again. I worked too hard and pretended I ate well. My blood pressure was through the roof. I kept that from you."

She wasn't going to let him distract her with his own puny sins. "You needed me. And then I left. Just like I did with Mom. And Grammy and Gramps."

"Lauren." His voice quieted. His fingers clenched hers. "When you were fourteen, did you know how to cure post-surgical infections?"

"No. Of course not," she admitted.

"And would you have stopped your grandparents from driving to Billings that day?"

"No. It's not about controlling what happens..."

"Then what is it about?"

"It's about making sure I'm here for you and Cadie and Andrew if something goes wrong."

"Cookie, you came home as fast as you could. We've

had some hard times as a family, but we've gotten through them together."

His assurance boosted her conviction. "Exactly. I need to stay so that we can keep facing stuff together."

"Lauren. That's not what I meant. We don't have to live in each other's pockets."

She shook her head, pulling her chair closer to the bed. Resting her head on his hand, she tried to believe him. And couldn't.

Her father, eyes tired, stroked her hair. "Would you expect me to cancel all my business trips or my annual Dublin vacation just in case you or Cadie or Andrew needed me?"

Agh, that makes sense. But it's different. She'd been the one to support her father, her sister, over the past year. If they didn't need her support, and if she didn't need to be a doctor for her mother's sake, then who was she, really?

"I'm afraid," she admitted.

"Of what?"

Dark spots formed behind her eyelids as she shut them hard enough to make her cheeks hurt. "Losing you. Mackenzie, Andrew, Cadie. Everyone."

"Tavish?" her dad asked quietly.

"Yeah." But she'd already lost him. Instead of working through her fears and taking the risk of compromising with him, her instinct had been to run away. Protecting them both. Except she hadn't protected him at all. She'd hurt him. And her clinical side shone a beacon into the hidden parts of her psyche, the ones she didn't want to look at. If a patient sat down in her office and told her a phobia was standing in the way of the person fully living life, Lauren would refer them to a counselor immediately. *Physician, heal thyself.*

"I don't know how to be with him. But we're not going to be able to completely sever ties." The alluding words came out before she thought about the fact her dad was hooked up to a half-dozen beeping machines. *Frick.* Getting big news hours after heart surgery wasn't in his best interest. She threw out a cover. "Because I love him."

Pain edged his smile. "You always have, Cookie."

"And it's never been enough, Dad."

"It's going to have to be, isn't it?" He glanced at the ceiling, then back at her. "I promised myself I wasn't going to compare you to your mother anymore. But I can't, not when it comes to this—she always got sick early in her first trimester."

"And…" she said, one last desperate attempt to evade the subject.

"Lauren—" his wan smile turned chiding "—you can't be retching in the bathroom all week at work without people noticing. Rumors made their way up the chain to me. I was going to wait for you to say something, but this morning reminded me that sometimes we shouldn't waste time."

Truth. She and Tavish had wasted so much time. A decade, really. Definitely the last year. "I'm pregnant, Dad."

"I know, Cookie. Which thrills me, truly. But how are you feeling about it?"

"About the baby? Fantastic." *The baby needs me.*

And Tavish said he needed her, too. But her meeting the baby's needs would mean not meeting Tavish's. Her inability to properly love the two people who were entitled to all she could give pinched her rib cage tight enough to steal her oxygen.

And she couldn't see a way to love them both without risking too much.

* * *

Mackenzie's "somewhere happier" involved navigating a warren of hospital hallways. Tavish strode behind her, surprised at her speed. She moved at a good clip for someone with a serious waddle. They emerged through a set of glass doors into a well-tended prayer garden. "Hopefully we won't have to be in a hospital again until I'm giving birth to this little one." She rubbed her belly and then her back. "Today's been pretty awful. Andrew's in shock."

"I could tell."

"And as much as I feel bad complaining when I'm not the one who just had a heart attack, my back is killing me. Being away, having time to ourselves was nice, but I'm so ready to have this baby."

"You got this, kiddo. Only four more weeks."

"Shh, don't tell Mackenzie," she joked in a theatrically quiet voice.

"You'll make it." He coughed. "Can't wait to meet him or her. I'm going to need the practice."

His sister reached for his arm and dug her short nails into his skin. "Practice?"

"Lauren's pregnant."

Mackenzie's eyebrows hit the sky. "No."

He cringed. "Crap. She didn't want to tell anyone yet."

She gave him a rib-cracking hug. "This is amazing! Your kid will be so close in age to mine! Cousin buddies. When did this happen? How?"

"When I was in town for the bachelor party. And the usual way." A smirk sneaked past the solemnity of the day.

"You're going to be a *daddy*. Holy jeez." Her smile faltered. "You must be crapping yourself."

He lifted a shoulder. "I'm feeling surprisingly calm about fatherhood, but pretty pessimistic about Lauren and me. She…she pushed me away today. Said she loved me too much to ask me to compromise any more than I already have."

"Sounds familiar," Mackenzie said grimly.

"Nothing like having your own horse crap flung back in your face."

A thoughtful hum passed through her closed lips. "You don't have to stay away."

"I know. I don't want to."

She startled. "You don't?"

Tavish paused, letting the scent of a nearby honeysuckle bush drift over him. He'd smelled the same fragrance yesterday on their hike, found it calming. Not so, today. If only he could go back twenty-four hours… *No.* Going backward never helped. He and Lauren needed to move forward. Together. It meant trying something entirely different on his part. For Lauren's sake, for the baby's, he'd stick. "I want to stay."

She nudged him with an elbow. "Have you told her how you feel?"

He bristled. "Yeah. She doesn't trust me. But a child? It's all-consuming, Kenz. I can't imagine wanting to go anywhere."

"I understand." Mackenzie's surprise softened into acceptance and sympathy. "It has a way of superseding everything."

The thought that had been lurking on the edges of his brain for a couple of weeks made it to his tongue. "So how could Dad have deserted us?"

A frown crossed his sister's face. "Immaturity. Selfishness. Bad choices. Take your pick."

"It was his nature." And Tavish was going to have to fight his own nature. He wouldn't give in like his father had.

"No, it was his choice. Just like it's yours. And you seem to be choosing the opposite."

"I'm trying to. But I've acted like him way too many times not to think that I inherited his tendencies."

She poked him in the chest. "You are not like Dad. He never wanted to be a parent. You do."

His mouth fell open. "He didn't want kids?"

Mackenzie served him a look of disbelief. "You thought he had? Why else would he have completely cut ties with us?"

"I'd never thought about it that closely." A lie. He had. He'd just ignored the answer, hadn't wanted to admit that his father didn't want him at all.

Acknowledging it now was no less of a shiv to the gut at thirty than at thirteen. The scenario he'd drawn for himself, of his dad being torn between wanting to be at home and wanting to get away, started to vanish into the ether of his childhood, replaced by the hard reality of complete rejection.

But the pain of analyzing his father's true feelings was followed by a flash of relief. If he was so different from his father on wanting children, he might be different on raising them, as well. The brick of genetics started to crumble inside him. He put a hand to his lightening chest. His stomach throbbed like he'd taken a gut shot. But it didn't itch with the need to flee.

Mackenzie stared at him with wide, compassionate eyes. "You'll be a great dad. And there's no reason you can't be with Lauren."

Oh, to be that confident. Despite the shift in his own

perspective, Lauren still stood in their way. "I can work on our trust problems, will stay in town for most of the year. But if she's still so ruled by fear and can't believe me, it'll hurt us over time. She pushed me away today. She said it was because she loved me and couldn't be what I needed, but I've said that way too many times myself to believe it."

Every time he'd spouted crap like that, it had been because he was afraid of something. Lauren claimed to be afraid of leaving her family. He didn't buy that anymore. She was afraid of people leaving her. And why wouldn't she be? Her mom, her grandparents—

Him.

Damn. Well, he'd prove her fears wrong this time. He wiped a hand down his face. His breath, thrashed by his nerves, came out jagged. He'd spent his whole life believing himself to be his father's replicate. Shifting away from that belief turned his self-image a hundred and eighty degrees. And if the arguments that had convinced him didn't convince Lauren…

He swore under his breath.

Mackenzie kicked him in the ankle.

"Ow. No one's in earshot."

"You're in a prayer garden. It's the principle of the thing." His sister's voice vibrated and her facial muscles twitched with what looked like pain. She swayed and her hands went to her belly.

He grabbed her around the waist and had to tense his arms to keep her upright. She was slowly becoming deadweight. Her knees must have given out. He shored her up against his side. "What's wrong?"

She hissed out a breath. "I think I'm having contractions."

He swore again. This time she didn't give him trouble over it. "You sure?"

Nodding so hard her whole upper body shook, she squeezed her eyes shut. "Yup. My water just broke."

Chapter Fifteen

Lauren clutched her dad's hand and watched him breathe long after he fell asleep again. She knew what he'd been trying to tell her. But even if he and Cadie and Andrew could live without her, the baby couldn't. Her little sprout—her heart panged at the memory of Tavish using the term—needed stability. Needed not to go through the agony that Lauren had experienced one too many times.

The door opened and Tavish stalled before entering the room, bracing his hand on the frame above his head. Concern stretched his skin tight to his jaw. "I need you, Pixie."

Her lip wobbled. "You said that. And I'm sorry, I can't—"

"Shh. That's not what I meant," he said, keeping his voice low. "Mackenzie's gone into labor. She's been having contractions all day, mistook it for a sore back. And she's begging for you. She's really worried about delivering early."

"Oh, God." Lauren shot to her feet. Grabbing his hand, she yanked him toward the nearest flight of stairs.

She'd been present for about twenty births—some as an intern, some as an attending—and she'd always found the delivery process sharpened her brain, making every part of the births clear in her mind.

Not so with Mackenzie's. The lack of official responsibility in the delivery took away the distinct sense of time. The hours blurred. Keeping Mackenzie calm. Keeping Andrew calm. Holding hands. Counting minutes between contractions.

For a first birth, and a premature one at that, Mackenzie's labor went fast. Intense, sure—she turned the air blue a few times—but no complications.

At three sixteen in the afternoon, Lauren breathed a sigh of relief. Her nephew's Apgar score was a nine out of ten, his lungs were developed, and aside from being a little small, there were no aftereffects of being born premature.

Her nugget of a nephew nestled against his mama under Andrew's watchful eye. Holy crap, Lauren was so the third wheel all of a sudden. Well, fourth.

"They're going to want to move you to a recovery room now, Kenz. I should go," she said.

Hair lank against her flushed face, Mackenzie sent Lauren an exhausted smile. "Thank you for being here."

"Thank you for letting me." She traced a finger down the cheek of her dad's new namesake. "You cooperate for your mama, okay, Teddy?"

She walked around to give Andrew a hug. "Congratulations, Daddy."

Despite the under-eye circles betraying his need for

sleep, her brother still managed to grip her with grizzly bear strength. "I didn't understand until I saw him, Laur, but wow. I'm going to give my boy the world. Just like Dad did for us."

Just like Dad. Give my boy the world.

Like every parent should do. She held on to her brother as shame weakened her knees. If she sheltered her child as she'd been doing herself, she'd be depriving the sprout in the worst way. Her brother glowed with devotion after all of fifteen minutes of parenthood. She'd feel the same way about her baby, would travel to Mongolia if it meant making him or her happy. And chances were, with half of Tavish's chromosomes, the kid would crave adventure.

Straightening, she stepped away from Andrew and took a centering breath. She would have to find a balance between settling and soaring. Doing so would mean a hell of a readjustment between her and the man lying two floors up in a hospital bed. Years of habitual guilt tried to rise, bubbling in her stomach.

Enough. Dad will be fine.

Her instincts didn't want to believe it, but she'd find a counselor who could give her strategies to deal with her fears. Untying herself from the burdens of her mother's and grandparents' deaths wasn't going to cause her to lose her good memories of them. And her family wasn't going to desert her if she wasn't there for them every moment. Her priorities needed to fully shift to creating a well-rounded life with the tiny being she was going to bring into the world, and to the man with whom she wanted to share each moment of parenthood.

Of everything.

"You'll be a fabulous father," she told her brother.

"And you'll be a fabulous mother," Mackenzie cut in.

Lauren stilled. Knowing smiles stretched both Mackenzie's and Andrew's faces. "You knew?"

"Tavish spilled the beans," Mackenzie explained. "But I got a little busy here, forgot to bring it up."

"I— Yeah. I'm seven weeks along."

"Amazing," Mackenzie said. Her expression went serious. "You'll be great together."

Lauren's stomach tumbled somewhere near the foot pedals of the adjustable bed. "I— Maybe. Instead of fighting for him, I told him to leave. I shouldn't have," she said in a rush when Andrew's eyebrows rose and Mackenzie's mouth firmed into a line. She took a deep breath. "And if he's headed for the airport again because of me being an idiot, I'll never forgive myself."

"Go find him. Talk to him. You'll figure it out." Laying a protective hand on her baby as he started to snuffle against her chest, Mackenzie shot Lauren a look hovering between cautious and hopeful. "Promise you'll listen to him."

Her friend's plea buoyed her. She would do more than listen to Tavish. She'd finally say the right thing.

Squinting against the bright primary colors of the maternity waiting room, Tavish pressed dial on his phone for the third time. Lauren had disappeared after their nephew had made his way into the world. He thought she'd returned to her dad's bedside, but nope. Nor was she answering her cell.

He hung up and gritted his teeth. Since when was she the one who took off? She'd started to apologize to him before he'd interrupted her with the news about Mackenzie—had he totally misread the situation? He'd assumed she'd meant *I'm sorry, I was wrong.* Maybe she'd still meant *I'm sorry, I can't do this*. The tendons in his neck tensed.

Where are you? he texted.

Her answer came quickly. I needed some fresh air.

His heart sank. Alone?

No. Come find me.

A picture of water rushing over her feet followed the invitation. Their river spot.

He sprinted for his car and broke a good dozen traffic laws while tearing down the highway to the trail that would lead him to the woman he needed more than the oxygen filling his lungs. By the time he emerged from the path into the clearing, his chest heaved from exertion.

Lauren sat on the log, swaying a little.

He rushed forward and braced his hands at her hips, supporting her slender frame. "Hey, there. Am I going to have to nag you to eat again?"

Settling against his arms, she shook her head. "I had a few energy bars. I'm just tired. Your sister, though. I've got nothing on her. What a heroine."

"You will be, too."

He straddled the log with her in between his knees. She drew her legs to her chest, leaned into him and hummed happily. Some of his tension seeped from his limbs. She wasn't proclaiming her undying love, but she definitely wasn't acting like someone who didn't want to be with him anymore. "You disappeared on me. I thought you'd gone to visit your dad, but he didn't have a clue where you were."

"He was fine. Aunt Georgie was there. And, like I said, I needed the fresh air."

Desperate that her willingness to leave her father's bedside meant she'd be willing to address the roots of what tied her so strongly to home, he flattened a palm against her belly. "I have a few things I need to tell you."

She shook her head. "Me first."

Being in Tavish's arms, soaking up his protection and possession, had to be the best feeling in the world. Loving him had never been the question. And now, she'd finally be able to compromise like he deserved.

Tipping and turning her head, she brushed a kiss along the underside of his jaw. The muscles clenched and released under her lips.

The shadows in his cheeks wavered between a smile and a grimace. God, she needed to erase all that uncertainty from the handsome features she intended to look at for the rest of her life. But where to start? Maybe with the simpler stuff. Ease in slowly.

"I'm starting to feel like a pretty big failure for not knowing what I want to do for a career," she admitted, letting the words betray the ache in her chest.

He stroked her back. "You'll find out a way to turn one of your hobbies into a job."

"I was thinking about how much I loved helping out the Canoe and Kayak Club with their athletic training back when I was in college. Had I not been so freaked of surgery, I would have probably gone into orthopedics. Maybe I can look into going back to school, get some more education and work at the new holistic health center like Cadie..."

"Just focus on finding something you find fulfilling," he said. "No one will think less of you if you take a few months to decide."

"I'll be showing by then. That'll limit my options."

Holding her head to his chest with a palm, he stayed silent.

Aching to fill the silence—to prevent her brain from churning itself into butter—she said, "Helping Mackenzie deliver made me think about my pregnancy a lot."

"I imagine it would," he murmured. "It's definitely been on my mind today."

Speaking of "on my mind..."

"Andrew said you never left the hospital. Even after I told you to go."

His eyes darkened. "I went for a walk. I wasn't going to desert you."

Right. Well. Staring at the water, she took a deep breath. The river faded from evergreen in the center to rusty rock on the edges. It teased the boulders in the middle, bubbling and gurgling in a calming way that completely belied her nerves. "I wanted to come here for a reason. I screwed up the last time we were here. And I need to make it right."

"Okay..."

After a deep breath, she found her courage. "When I was in the delivery room and saw Andrew holding Teddy like the little guy was one of Mom's Venetian glass Christmas ornaments—" Taking one of his hands, she toyed with his callused fingers. "And I mean, I've seen that infinite-parental-love look before, many times in the delivery room, but this time, it was different. So different. That'll be me soon. Us. And when Andrew said he'd give his son the world... I want to be that, do that, for our baby. With you."

A breeze brushed across her skin, threatened to topple the emotional house of cards on which she teetered. She forced her fingers to still and stared at him straight-on. "Ask me. Ask me what you asked me the last time we were here."

His fingers twisted around hers. "I don't want to ask that anymore."

A vise clamped around her chest, turned one notch. "You have to. Please. Believe me. I'll give the right answer."

His slow blink, his rapid lip lick, turned the vise once more. "Lauren… I already believe you. It's all over your face. But I don't need that answer from you anymore. I don't need to know you'll come with me."

"But…" Disappointment clawed back the hope that had started to fill the cracks in her heart. She swallowed. "I thought that's what you wanted."

"It was." He slowly caressed her cheek with his palm. "But as much as you've changed, so have I. I need to know that if I tell you I intend to stay here—for good, with you, with our baby—that you'll trust me. That the issue of my job, or my past tendency to get gone, won't keep coming back. We couldn't live with that haunting us for the rest of our lives."

She owed him not to placate, not to give him the knee-jerk *Of course I trust you* that wanted to rip from her lungs.

"What changed?" she asked.

"The same thing that changed you. I want to give our baby every opportunity possible." His voice was so low, so gravel-filled and raw, she could barely hear him. Picking up a flat, river-polished stone and rolling it between the flattened fingers of both his hands, he flicked it at the water. It skipped once, twice, three times before sinking. Inhaling deeply, he continued.

"The last time we were here…we'd just made love. You wanted to stay. And all I wanted was to get the hell out—not away from you, or away from our relationship, but out of Sutter Creek."

She remembered that. His tense jaw, so handsome but so wrecked. His fraught plea. *Love me enough to come with me.*

Now, she loved him enough to go anywhere.

But more than that, she loved herself enough to allow her to go. Loved her family enough to know they'd support her in that decision.

And the contrast between Tavish's face today and his face the last time they'd been here was as clear as the water rushing past their feet. All panic, gone. All skittishness, gone.

And, most importantly, he wasn't gone.

"You want to stay," she breathed.

"Damn right, I do. I'm not my father. And I promise you I'll never become him." The gravity in his expression, not sad-serious, but one that acknowledged the profundity of the situation while still sparkling with anticipation, solidified her shaky foundation.

She knew Tavish. And he was telling God's honest truth. Every molecule in his body projected a singular message: he wasn't going anywhere.

Not now, not ever.

"I trust you." The dregs of fear melted into the log and down into the sand at her feet as she burrowed into his embrace. "And I'll be happy with one child, so that we can stay more portable."

He shook his head. "I want a big family. We can work on turning that house of yours into a home of ours. I spent my twenties running all over the world. My thirties will be about creating my own—our own—world. You. Me. Kids. Our parents and siblings and nieces and nephews." He reached into his back pocket and pulled out his passport. "I've always carried this on me. Take it. Safeguard it. Our children are going to need stability."

She took it from his hand and slipped it back into his pocket. "No. You hang on to it. Yeah, kids need stability, Tav. But they need wonder, too."

"Then let's give them both. Starting with parents who love and are committed to each other." He shifted her out of his lap and knelt in the sand, looking up at her in earnest. "Will you marry me, Lauren? Again?"

"Yes." A wave of unstoppable joy erupted, shimmering perfection throughout every pore of her skin. "Yes!"

He unfastened his bracelet and linked it onto her wrist, threading the toggle through a middle link to make it fit. The loose end dragged against the back of her hand. She stroked the center links, the rings they'd exchanged last summer. "We can have these reshaped into bands."

Surprise lit his features. He rose, sat and pulled her onto his lap again. "You don't want to start fresh?"

"No." Letting the warmth of the sun, and of Tavish's love, sink in, she pressed her lips to the corner of his mouth, then tilted over and took his mouth in a full, sensuous kiss. "Our past has made us just as much as our present and our future. I want to be rid of the barriers that have kept us apart, but I still want to hang on to the love I had for you then. It's just a matter of building on it. Of creating our home together."

"Home's wherever you are, sweetheart. And I've never wanted to have it so much."

Epilogue

Fourteen months later

Lauren smoothed a hand up her infant daughter's straining back. Points to her sister for swearing Ben sensed his mommy's anxiety. It sure seemed to be the same for Charlotte. All the misery in the world was screwed into her tiny, teary face. Lauren's heart ached with guilt at the same time it jittered with nerves.

"I'm sorry, sweetheart," she whispered, bobbing around the kitchen island. "Shh."

"I'll get her calm. And you, too." Hips resting against the counter, Tavish tugged at Lauren's upper arm until both she and Charlotte were encircled by strong muscles. His wide palm rested on Charlotte's back, working its magic as usual. The baby's snuffles turned happy, and she nuzzled into Lauren's chest.

"I shouldn't be going back to school so soon," she

squeaked, melting into her husband's embrace. "Charlotte's barely six months old—what if she gets hungry, or starts crying or..."

Tavish's lips curved against Lauren's cheek. "If she gets hungry, I'll feed her. If she cries, I'll find a way to make her stop. And in three hours, when your classes are over, you can come back and make sure I've done a good job."

His words slowed her pulse from a sprint to a jog. "You're so fricking good at being a daddy. And a husband," she added in a rush.

He toyed with her finger, rubbed his thumb against the gold band he'd put there last New Year's Eve. Nine months later and it felt like the ring was a part of her. If only it didn't feel like she was sawing off a limb by leaving her daughter to upgrade her health education coursework, and everything would be back to normal. But she needed to take this step. She'd worked at the holistic health center from when it opened last fall until Charlotte's birth, and she wanted to take the exam to become a Community Health Education Specialist, which meant upgrading her degrees with some sociology credits.

"How about I play chauffeur?" he offered. "I'll take Charlie and she can nap in my office."

Tavish had gone from artist-in-residence at Montana State to sessional instructor within two semesters. His classes had filled up quicker than any other photography course. Lauren had been tempted to take one herself, but it didn't quite fit in with her program. Plus, she could get private lessons from the most in-demand instructor on campus any time she wanted.

"Okay," she said sheepishly. "I'll drive myself on Friday, I promise. These are just first-day jitters."

"Pixie, I'll drive you anywhere, anytime. In fact, how

does bypassing school, driving on to New York City sound?" he said, clearly teasing.

"That would completely waste the tickets we have booked for our anniversary," she scolded.

"I can't wait to take you up Rockefeller Center." His eyes lit as they started to get the diaper bag ready for their daughter. "But promise me we'll come right back home?"

"If you want."

Utter seriousness, blended with utter contentment, set his eyes a deep violet. "I have everything I want right here. No place in the world could ever compare."

* * * * *

Don't miss Zach and Cadie's story,
coming in 2019 from Harlequin Special Edition!

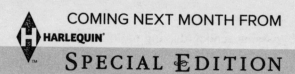

COMING NEXT MONTH FROM

HARLEQUIN®

SPECIAL EDITION

Available March 20, 2018

#2611 FORTUNE'S FAMILY SECRETS
The Fortunes of Texas: The Rulebreakers • by Karen Rose Smith
Nash Fortune Tremont is an undercover detective staying at the Bluebonnet Bed and Breakfast. Little does he know, the woman he's been spilling his secrets to has some of her own. When Cassie's secrets come to light, will their budding relationship survive the lies?

#2612 HER MAN ON THREE RIVERS RANCH
Men of the West • by Stella Bagwell
When widow Katherine O'Dell literally runs into rancher Blake Hollister on the sidewalk, she's not looking for love. She and her son have already come second to a man's career, but Blake is determined to make them his family and prove to Katherine that she'll always be first in his heart.

#2613 THE BABY SWITCH!
The Wyoming Multiples • by Melissa Senate
When Liam Mercer, a wealthy single father, and Shelby Ingalls, a struggling single mother, discover their babies were switched at birth, they marry for convenience...and unexpectedly fall in love!

#2614 A KISS, A DANCE & A DIAMOND
The Cedar River Cowboys • by Helen Lacey
Fifteen years ago, Kieran O'Sullivan shattered Nicola Radici's heart and left town. Now he's back—and if her nephews have their way, wedding bells might be in their future!

#2615 FROM BEST FRIEND TO DADDY
Return to Stonerock • by Jules Bennett
After one night of passion leads to pregnancy, best friends Kate McCoy and Gray Gallagher have to navigate their new relationship and the fact that they each want completely different—and conflicting—things out of life.

#2616 SOLDIER, HANDYMAN, FAMILY MAN
American Heroes • by Lynne Marshall
Mark Delaney has been drifting since returning home from the army. When he meets Laurel Prescott, a widow with three children who's faced struggles of her own, he thinks he might have just found the perfect person to make a fresh start with.

YOU CAN FIND MORE INFORMATION ON UPCOMING HARLEQUIN® TITLES, FREE EXCERPTS AND MORE AT WWW.HARLEQUIN.COM.

HSECNM0318

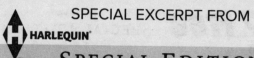

SPECIAL EXCERPT FROM

HARLEQUIN®

SPECIAL EDITION

*Single parents Liam Mercer and Shelby Ingalls just
found out their little boys were switched in the hospital
six months ago! Will they find a way to stay in the lives
of both boys they've come to love?*

Read on for a sneak preview of
THE BABY SWITCH!
the first book in the brand-new series
THE WYOMING MULTIPLES
by **Melissa Senate**, *also known as Meg Maxwell!*

"Are you going to switch the babies back?"

Shelby froze.

Liam felt momentarily sick.

It was the first time anyone had actually asked that
question.

"No, ma'am," Liam said. "I have a better idea."

Shelby glanced at him, questions in her eyes.

"Where is my soup!" Kate's mother called again.

"You go ahead, Kate," Shelby said, stepping out onto the
porch. "Thanks for talking to us."

Kate nodded and shut the door behind them.

Liam leaned his head back and he started down the porch
steps. "I need about ten cups of coffee or a bottle of scotch."

"I thought I might fall over when she asked about
switching the babies back," Shelby said, her face pale, her
green eyes troubled. She stared at him. "You said you had
a better idea. What is it? I sure need to hear it. Because
switching the babies is not an option. Right?"

HSEEXP0318

"Damned straight it's not. Never will be. Shane is your son. Alexander is my son. No matter what. Alexander will also become your son and Shane will also become my son as the days pass and all this sinks in."

"I think so, too," she said. "Right now it's like we can't even process that babies we didn't know until Friday are ours biologically. But as we begin to accept it, I'll start to feel a connection to Alexander. Same with you and Shane."

He nodded. "Exactly. Which is why on the way here, I started thinking about a way to ease us into that, to give us both what we need and want."

She tilted her head, waiting.

He thought he had the perfect solution. The only solution.

"I called the lab running the DNA tests and threw a bucket of money at them to expedite the results. On Monday," he continued, "we will officially know for absolute certain that our babies were switched. Of course we're not going to switch them back. I'd sooner cut off my arm."

"Me, too," Shelby said, staring at him. "So what's your plan?"

"The plan is for us to get married."

Shelby's mouth dropped open. "What? We've been living together for a day. Now we're getting married. Legally wed? Till death do us part?"

Don't miss
THE BABY SWITCH! by Melissa Senate,
available April 2018 wherever
Harlequin® Special Edition books and ebooks are sold.

www.Harlequin.com

THE WORLD IS BETTER
WITH
Romance

Harlequin has everything from contemporary, passionate and heartwarming to suspenseful and inspirational stories.

Whatever your mood,
we have a romance just for you!

Connect with us to find your next great read,
special offers and more.

f /HarlequinBooks

@HarlequinBooks

www.HarlequinBlog.com

www.Harlequin.com/Newsletters

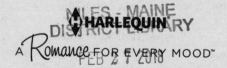

HARLEQUIN

A Romance FOR EVERY MOOD™

www.Harlequin.com

SERIESHALOAD2015